IRIS AFTER THE INCIDENT

MINA V. ESGUERRA

BRIGHT GIRL BOOKS

This book is a work of fiction. Names, characters, places, and incidents are products of the author's imagination or are used fictitiously. Any resemblance to actual events or locales or persons, living or dead, is entirely coincidental.

Iris After the Incident

Copyright © 2016 Mina V. Esguerra. All rights reserved.

Cover designed by Tania Arpa

Photography by Pach Urrea

Visit instagram.com/romanceclasscovers

Xander: You have no shame.
Cordelia: Oh please. Like shame is something to be proud of.
— Buffy the Vampire Slayer, "Earshot"

ONE

Apart from evaluating your documents, we will need an essay that will allow us to get to know you, as a person. What are your special talents, Iris Len-Larioca? Please state your answer in 500 words or less.

WITH ONE LOOK, I can detect a specific kind of pervert.

I've become a pervert detector.

Not something I was proud of.

I'm sure someone else in the world would find that talent useful. Maybe people in forensics, in international law enforcement...who actually needed to find the truly depraved and take them out of society. But I didn't have that kind of skill anyway. My accidental talent seemed to cover only the borderline harmless.

The silver lining there was that it only took a moment to know that I didn't need a person in my life. *Not you, not you, not your brother, not your perv dad.* People thought they learned something new about me, but this mirror had two faces, and it showed me yours as much as it showed you mine.

Relax, and don't think of it that way, my therapist said. *You're an attractive person. Attractive people get looked at. It's not always for the reason you think it is.*

It was hard to believe her, but eventually I almost, kind of, did. The reason I kept visiting Janine, the third therapist I saw after The Incident, was because of her firm position that humanity was not doomed, people had a lot of good in them, and there was no sense hiding under a rock.

For the most part, it helped. Helped me get through the day, and accomplish the stupidly simple thing of going across the street to buy toothpaste. You know how messed up it can be, when you start Googling "baking soda toothpaste recipe" so you don't have to dress up, go out, and cross the street? I mean, I did that for a while and told myself it was because I was in a DIY phase but…yeah. I was afraid of going to the convenience store.

And everywhere else.

Janine's support helped me through that, and while I'm truly over it and can buy groceries now, sometimes I feel eyes on me and I know.

I know. *Pervert.*

The Incident was two years ago, and I'm fine now. Mostly. I said that when Janine and I last met, maybe four months ago. We had begun meeting less and less.

Great, she'd said. *Because you did nothing wrong, and you know what the next step is, right?*

What's that? I had asked.

Back to normal.

A *new* normal, we'd both agreed. Certain things weren't ever coming back, and they shouldn't be coming back anyway.

The unexpected silver lining of The Incident was that it trimmed away so much of my life's excesses. People especially, who weren't the best for me, and then suddenly, they were gone. Poof! Those and a few things could stay gone.

I knew what Janine meant, though.

How do I know when I'm ready? I'd asked her.

No one is, she'd said. *No one's ever ready for life to completely change again.*

IRONICALLY, I was the calm one, that day when the elevator stopped.

Blue-Eyed Boy was *not* calm. Sure, he was trying to be, but when the elevator remained stalled between floors five and six for more than a few seconds, those eyes stopped looking up at the frozen display screen and then landed on me.

"Does this happen a lot?" he asked, and he sounded Filipino, which surprised me a little. I mean, blue eyes. I saw him in the building a few times, and I knew we both lived on the ninth floor. Then it occurred to me that I'd never *heard* him, and always assumed that if I did, he'd have some kind of American accent. West Coast.

I had no evidence to support that, apparently. He could have been from anywhere, because handsome guys with dark hair and blue eyes could have come from anywhere. He could have grown up anywhere too, and it sounded like he grew up right here.

Two years of silently asking people not to judge me, and I hadn't turned it around and fixed that setting in myself.

Good job, Iris.

"No," I said, and I was surprised that my reaction was to

try and be comforting. It was just the two of us in there, and maybe it reminded me of my therapy sessions. Maybe I was done with being the person who needed help. "I mean, I've been living here definitely over a year and it's never happened. They did announce that they were doing tests of the electrical system for something."

"They did?" Blue-Eyed Boy's voice was nice, but this probably wasn't his normal one. It was straining to sound casual. He didn't realize this but the vulnerability was cute, also the attempt to hide it. "Shit. I never read the memos."

The lights above us flickered, and flickered again, and then stayed on.

I laughed. "Okay that might be it."

He looked up at the display, which said "five," but we still weren't moving.

I should have been nervous, but I wasn't. Looking back now, maybe I should have been, because we could have been stuck there for hours. The power could have gone out for longer and for worse reasons. But maybe I too was trying to stay calm and collected for the sake of Blue Eyes.

"Should we hit the emergency thing?" he said, but he was looking at the yellow round button with a bell on it, not me. And then he just did it, anyway.

We paused, and nothing.

"Hmm." It was eleven p.m., and by this time the security staff were down to the night shift crew and I assumed there wouldn't be as many people around. But there would definitely be someone at the lobby. I had my work bag with me though, and pulled out a notepad and pen.

HELLO! HELP PLS. 9M HERE. I wrote, running through the letters several times to make the writing darker. Then I held up the little sign against the security camera that I knew was on the upper right corner.

"Oh, nice," Blue Eyes said.

"Someone should be watching the monitors, at least," I added, "even if they don't hear the alarm or whatever it is that button does."

The speaker on the panel beside us buzzed to life. "Hello. Thank you for alerting us. There's a talk button on this panel, please press it once so we can hear you."

"Hi," I said, doing just that. "Can you hear me? Is this Gordon?"

"Yes, ma'am. We're sorry about this. They began to test the electrical system and it affected elevator 4 but we should have made sure all elevators were empty. We're switching back on now and you'll be on your way in two minutes. Is anyone else there with you, ma'am?"

"9J," Blue Eyes said.

"We're sorry. Please stand by."

"Thank you very much," I said.

We both backed away from the speaker and...had nowhere else to go. It was hard to not look at each other though, because all four walls of the elevator were reflective surfaces. If I looked one way, I would see his eyes, the nice shape of his lips. The sweep of his hair up and to the left, revealing a worried forehead. The other wall reflected an image of his broad back, straight and rigid because he was looking up, waiting for the display to change. A little lower down that wall and I could check out how his butt curved in his jeans, and...

No no no, don't go there, Iris.

I kept my eyes straight ahead and instead just saw myself.

"Two minutes," he said. "God it feels longer."

"Do enclosed spaces bother you?" *Did you just talk to him like you were a therapist? No don't do that either, Iris!*

"I never thought about it before," he said. "But maybe. And...and that was cool that you had pen and paper with you, because I don't have anything."

"I have too many things in my bag. At least some things are useful."

"I don't even have a phone," he said. "Isn't that stupid? I stopped bringing one around and now I'm so used to it. Then this happens and I have nothing to use to call for help."

Oh. That *would* make someone worried, in this situation. But that was a strange thing to admit, in this day and age. No phone? Off the grid? Was he trying to be old school or hipster or something?

Don't judge, I reminded myself. Because maybe he was hiding.

I understood that.

"Well," I said, "they monitor all the elevators. They would have gotten us out even if we didn't ask."

He was deep in thought, and when I said that, he looked at me like he had come back from a faraway place. "Well, of course. I should know that. I chose this building because of the security and shit. It's just...I don't know. It feels stupid now to not have any way to contact people."

I shrugged. "It goes both ways, I guess. If you can reach out, then you can be reached too."

"Yeah," he said. "Maybe I should stop worrying about that."

The display changed, and finally became "six." Then "seven." And then the doors opened on the ninth floor, home, and we stepped on solid ground at nearly the same time.

"Oh my god," I said, finally letting some emotion out. "I'm glad that wasn't *so* bad."

"Thank you. Yeah, for the sign, and talking to the guards."

I smiled. "No problem. Good night, 9J."

Blue Eyes blinked, and then smiled back at me. "Right. Good night and thank you, 9M."

We took off in different directions. I may have been smiling as I let myself into apartment 9M of Tower 3, at the NV Park complex, I couldn't be sure. It might have been the first time in a long time that I did that.

The other thing? He looked at me, and it was *normal*. It felt like it.

Maybe this "new normal" could work out after all.

TWO

Funny how things turn out sometimes.

I happened to be coming home from work at eleven p.m.—the right time to get stuck in there with 9J—because that was my work schedule now. Unofficially. After the Incident, I almost quit my job at the foundation I worked for. The main thing that it did was manage a scholarship fund for female STEM (science, technology, engineering, mathematics) students. At that time, I was being sent to meetings with sponsors, institutions, affluent donors, and schools willing to work on the cause. Then, rather abruptly, I couldn't go out to meet them anymore. My bosses understood that, and didn't force me to either.

They kept me on because there was more work to be done that didn't require seeing people. Letters had to be written, presentations had to be made pretty, and spreadsheets needed updating. I wasn't much of a writer or researcher, but had to learn because I became the work-from-home person, and then, starting this year, the desk-job person. I needed some help with the transition back to the office, and they allowed me to work flexible hours. I avoided the normal day shift; came in late, and left work very late. Even as I became more comfortable going out again, I stuck to that schedule.

At least they didn't let me quit, thank god. It would have been worse to have ended up broke after The Incident. The firm was founded by a brother and sister team, Carl and Miley Figueras, and they rejected the five resignation letters I sent. Each time I was completely sincere about it, and three of those times, it was because I felt that *they* were getting into trouble because of me, and that leaving was the selfless thing for me to do.

Miley asked for a meeting at six p.m., which to me was like lunch (as in middle of my work day), while she was on her way out. She was my only boss now; Carl left the firm last year, moved to the United States to get married. It had been a difficult decision for him, leaving the "baby" that was his company, but no one blamed him. He wouldn't have been able to marry here, and he didn't have to chain himself to this place forever.

"We're almost done with the brochures we're sending to the fair in Cebu," I said, as soon as I sat down on the chair across from her. "The background color was off and the entire back flap was so hard to read, so I asked them to redo it."

"Oh there's time. No worries," she said, and maybe the first thing I should have noticed was that she was watching me as soon as I walked into her office. Miley Figueras was usually busy whenever one saw her, and she didn't have her eye on her phone or laptop screen at all when we started.

I should have guessed.

"Iris," she said, "I'm moving."

I knew what that meant. Carl said that too—*I'm moving*. When they said that, it didn't mean they were getting a house in Nuvali or leasing a two-bedroom in Taguig. It meant another kind of moving. Far, and permanent.

I tried not to let it show on my face that my insides felt like they were imploding.

"Wow," I said. "To where?"

"Switzerland," Miley said. "That project in Geneva. It's a great opportunity."

"Congratulations." They were a former client, a grant-giving foundation, and they did like her work. No surprise they would have wanted her to join them, and no surprise that she'd say yes.

"Thank you. I kind of didn't want to start from scratch as someone's employee somewhere, but when am I going to be considered young enough to do this, right?"

Miley was in her mid-thirties and wasn't old to me at all, but I knew what she meant. I was twenty-four and The Incident made me feel like I had started over. She wanted to try to do the life change while she had the stamina. We talked about starting over a lot, way more than coworkers should.

I knew this would happen. She had hinted it would, when Carl left. Their firm was still relatively small, despite being around for ten years. Just them, me, half a dozen other people.

"Right now you're the most senior here, at least in terms of the actual operations work," she said. "A happy accident, because you were both in marketing and in operations. No one else has done both sides like that, apart from me and Carl. So if you're ready, you can lead the project teams. All of them."

Wow. What?

Was I actually getting promoted?

I tried to think of other people who would be better at this than me. The nature of the firm though was to keep a small full-time staff, and hire consultants for anything else. Among the staff, my three years and college internship was indeed the longest anyone has ever been working there.

Miley cleared her throat. "But what the firm needs is new partners, all the time, Iris. You know that. And it would be best if the person who knows the work best was also the one meeting them and answering questions."

"I don't know about this," was my automatic answer.

"You really don't? You don't think enough time has passed?"

"But we agreed," I said. Miley had let me stay away from shaking any hands so the firm's reputation would remain good and intact. "This is *the opposite* of that."

"Iris, I don't want to bring things up but no one has mentioned it in...I don't even remember. We haven't lost any partners recently because your name was part of the employee list."

She was right. But two years ago, they did. Some high-profile donors and institutions deferred working with us. Every time someone did, I sent a resignation letter.

Miley shrugged. "Not asking you to do anything you don't want to do. But when I leave, and my dad takes over here, you know he's just going to want numbers."

Carl and Miley's dad was part owner of the firm and without the two, he'd be the boss of us. I wasn't sure what that meant for me; it had been his son and daughter who had stuck by me. "Does he care about...?"

"He wasn't happy about it, but everyone keeps their jobs if they're useful. And he's going to want people to be extra useful. Do you get what I mean?"

It meant that the Figueras patriarch had other businesses and didn't care much for the well-meaning startup his kids put up, except maybe to keep the lights on, and see it earn more.

"I'll have to think about this," I said. "But congratulations. I really am happy for you."

Miley nodded. "I know you mean that, and thanks. And...I should let you know that Francine called again."

I must have looked like I spaced out.

"Francine Porter of—"

"I know, I know," I said, cutting her off. Francine Porter's non-profit agency was a partner of ours. "Is there—why?"

"You know. The usual. They're doing a seminar and she asked again if you would meet with her."

Again my answer was automatic. "Oh. Okay. Can you email me the details?"

I always said that, and I never acted on it. Email was the black hole of asking me to talk to Francine. The only time I would do it was if I were trapped in an elevator with her, maybe.

But it was easier to say I would, and then not do it, than explain why I wouldn't.

My boss was skeptical, but as always, careful about this. "She really does believe in your work. She actually wants to offer you a job with them. Full time."

"What?"

"You haven't thought of it?" Miley asked. "They say your generation gets tired of a job after three years or less."

Not when you've been the kindest to me of everyone in this mess. "Are you asking me to quit?"

Miley sighed. Then she laughed. "Of course not."

This was messed up. My own boss acting as my career

scout. But again, it was easier to say I would consider it, rather than talk about all the reasons.

"Email that to me too," I said. *And off into the black hole it goes.*

"Of course." And yet Miley was looking straight at me when she said this, made no move to type anything up. "I will. When you're ready, you can do a lot for them. As their employee or just...you."

"I have work to do," I mumbled, and that was my way of excusing myself.

YOU CAN DO a lot for them.

I knew that, in my head. I knew that because my job had me contacting experts and getting them to write, review, check stuff, to make our work better and more useful. *Useful* was the key word, and everything we did had to be that. I couldn't blame Francine for calling, and asking. This was probably the third time.

She wanted my help because her non-profit provided counseling services to underprivileged women and children, and The Incident that happened to me was becoming something they needed...information on.

Ugh. "The Incident." Calling it that in my head shielded me from having to remember, but it also created walls in my memory, head places I instinctively felt I couldn't go to.

After work, on a normal day, I would be home by eleven. I'd have a takeout dinner with me. I would sit there and watch something on TV for a few hours, and then I'd sleep.

Today, same routine, but I also toyed with some

thoughts. I wondered if I could say it out loud, even when by myself. I realized that I'd never actually done that. Janine never made me.

So I sat there on my living room couch, dinner done, cup of hot tea brewing, and dared myself to say it.

Or just think it, in a complete sentence.

Which moment has most defined your life so far, Iris Len-Larioca? Please state your answer in 500 words or less.

I could do that.

I had sex with my boyfriend.

And we took a video.

And it accidentally got out on the internet.

People saw it.

Short, heavy sentences. Even as silent thoughts.

I braced myself for all the feelings that thinking about it brought on, especially in the beginning. And…it was there. Kind of? A little. The pain was familiar, but not as devastating.

"That's right." I said that aloud, first as a whisper. "That was me. I was the naked girl on the internet."

That wasn't a joke. It was bitter in my mouth, and bitter in the air. It was also true.

But then I had to get up and throw my takeout carton away. And throw the trash into the chute down the hall. And wash the cup I'd used. Like any other day, like always.

THREE

A few days after the thing with the elevator, I got home to find a piece of paper on my floor, pushed in from under my door.

Thank you again for being the sane one. If you want to hang out in a wider space, you know where to find me.

Signed: *9J*.

Was I actually going to do this? I hadn't dated at all in two years. Well, a year and a half, because technically Bradley and I didn't break up for some time after the In— after the video of us went online. By that final month we were barely speaking, and he had already packed up and moved to his sister's in Maryland. Moving to the US where he had family had always been an option for him, but at the time we'd only been dating a year and his future didn't seem like it had to be mine just yet.

Earlier into the drama, he made that his plan A. An escape plan, that could include me, except it was a little too complicated. I didn't want to just suddenly marry him, uproot myself, and start over (there's that again) somewhere else. First of all, it was the internet, and they had that in the

US too, duh. The only thing he'd escape would be the looks of crushing disappointment he was getting from the people he knew here.

I told him they would forget. I mean, who remembered last month's internet scandal anymore? No one. I told him to hang on, and we'd get through it. That he wasn't even going to get the worst of the hate, because he was the guy and people expected him to not just have sex, but have folders of obscene stuff everywhere. If anyone was going to get branded a scarlet letter (what would it be, an "S"?), it would be me.

"Then you should want this more than I do," he'd said, during an argument about Maryland. "I'm giving you a way out, Iris."

I wanted a lot of things. There was a wish list: To go back in time and not have pressed the red button that started the recording. To have the power to keep work laptops from ever crashing. To make an app that automatically deleted a private video as soon as a stranger's eyes looked at it. So many things.

Still, not including what seemed like an offer to elope to save me from shame.

Bradley used to like my sense of humor, by the way. But this had gotten to him in a way I didn't expect. Then again, you can't predict how people will react when their most private acts are exposed.

So, anyway. No dates in two years. Because in the beginning I was too sensitive about what they might have known, and what they might have wanted.

Also, I stopped getting asked out. Truth.

I turned the piece of paper over and wrote *Saturday*. Then, *Dinner, 7 PM*. Then, *I'll pick you up. Y/N?*

Writing that down was a breakthrough. The next one

would be to actually open my door, walk down the hall, turn the corner toward his side of the tower, and slide the note back to him.

Screw it, I said. I signed the note 9M and stepped out into the hall, before I could tell myself that this was a bad idea. Because maybe it wasn't. Maybe I was ready for this, to go out with someone, and maybe he would be one of the first guys to look at me like normal. Why the hell not.

I might have skipped like a happy little girl, during those last few steps. It felt like I was claiming something. Which was silly; this was the equivalent of leaving a note inside a locker. It wasn't as brave or as legendary as I was making it out to be.

9J. Hello there. I bent down, slipped the paper underneath the door, and broke into a jog back to my unit.

"Hey!"

Holy shit. I froze at the sound of his voice.

"Hey," he said, again, and he sounded closer.

Turning around wasn't so hard. I had to. It was the proper thing to do, after sliding a note under someone's apartment door. When I turned around and saw him again: dark hair, blue eyes. Every part of his face nicely proportioned. Dark bangs hung down his forehead, something that wasn't part of his look last time, and it made him seem younger. Like a naughty boy. I had forgotten how I was into that, and probably contributed to the mess that I was just getting myself out of. This part, this wasn't so easy.

Being "just a girl" again.

I cleared my throat. "Hello," I said, all formal. "Um, yeah. I replied."

He was holding the piece of paper. He was also wearing baggy pajama pants and...he wasn't wearing a shirt. Of course. It was almost midnight, and normal people were sleeping at this hour. 9J was probably about to go to bed. He probably didn't like wearing shirts in bed. Ah, crap.

"Yes," he said.

"Yeah?" Damn, 9J took care of himself. I mean, I suspected that, because even with clothes on he looked *firm*. Nicely shaped. Like he'd be the type who'd use the open field in the NV Park complex to kick balls and stuff. Or use the roof deck patio to do sit-ups.

"I mean, yes. Lunch on Saturday. Where do you want to go?"

Oh. Well. At first it was difficult not to gawk at his eyes, and then I had to avoid staring at his bare chest, but the question threw me yet again. My instinct was to think of one of the smaller restaurants, and nearby, stay within the neighborhood, didn't want to go out in public…

"I'll cook," I said. "But let's eat poolside. Here, Tower 3."

"Oh," he said, and he looked relieved. "Interesting. I didn't think of that. Yes. Poolside would be awesome. And you cook? Great. Let's do that."

"Great," I said. "Please…go back inside. I'm sorry, it's late."

"Not a problem." His smile was shy, almost surprising on that face which was on that head and on that body. "I guess I'll see you on Saturday, 9M."

"Good night," I told him. "9J."

I turned and started back toward my side of the tower, but didn't hear the sound of his door clicking shut.

"We're really doing this?" he called out. "You're not going to tell me your name?"

I was about to turn the corner and was relieved that I had a wall I could hide behind. I wasn't sure how to deal with this, which face to put on, because I had a face for the people who only pretended not to know, and it would probably make me appear unkind.

Pause. Step back. Turn around.

I smiled at him. "You haven't told me yours."

Then it was like he did a version of the exact thing I did. He too seemed to take a second to decide what to do. Like he was bracing himself for a jump.

He smiled at me. "Fair enough. Good night, and see you on Saturday, 9M."

NEW FRIENDSHIPS WERE hard to come by as well, after The Incident. Although Matilda from the fourteenth floor was the notable exception.

I moved into NV Park about a year and a half ago; before that, I was still living at home with my parents and brother. The building swimming pool was now my go-to fitness option. I became aware of when it was used the least, so when my avoiding-people phase was at its height, and I didn't want to go to the gym or even run around the complex, I used the pool. Saturdays, noon and right after, was the best time for me to use it. A little earlier in the morning and there would be a lot of kids there. Later in the afternoon, and the older residents, at least the non-toddler types, were hanging out, using the free Wi-Fi. Noon was when the sun was its most unbearable, and because of how the pool area was designed, people avoided being there at that time.

So that was my time. Me time. I became the girl who used the pool at noon, and even when people showed up, they kept to themselves. When I first moved here, I worried about how sociable people would be, if they expected me to smile and be friendly. I did smile, and I was friendly when I had to be, but so far no one forced me to be friends with them.

There's comfort in being anonymous, just another person in the crowd, Janine had said, when I told her that I felt more comfortable now living among strangers in a small apartment, than with my actual family in a roomy house. *At home you have space, but only physical. Everyone else is in your head, your business, your history.*

The New Normal involved more strangers, that was true. It didn't involve the gym anymore though, because I didn't enjoy doing that anyway, so I let that go.

Unfortunately, I also had to let go of the friends I thought I had. Maybe it was my fault—I only had a few, a core group of friends I'd been close to since we were pre-teens. They were both already married, already mothers, and they were mortified when the thing happened to me. Not for me, but mortified, period.

Matilda began using the pool around the same time as my "me time" several months after I'd moved to NV Park. I noticed her right away because she was there at the same time every day all of a sudden. On the third consecutive day of no longer doing my swim alone, she'd spoken up.

"Sorry," she'd said. "You're Iris Len-Larioca, right?"

"Yeah," I'd replied, grabbing my towel. She sounded and acted like she would be my age, but looked a little older. Not because she looked *old*, but there was something almost too glamorous and knowing about her. "Do I know you from somewhere?"

"I used to live here, but you probably moved in while I was away. I'm back now. I'm Matilda Ruiz."

"Hello," I'd said, not sure what she was talking about. She was wearing a shiny gold bikini, and she looked beautiful and confident. Was she a celebrity? Was I supposed to know who she was?

"I don't want to freak you out, but I want to tell you this because it matters to me. I admire you. I know what happened, and I admire how you've gone on with your life after."

Oh.

"Um, thank you," I'd said. Not that she would know anything about my life, but I was obviously alive and healthy and swimming in the pool in front of her. "That means a lot."

I wasn't ready for a new friend at the time, so I excused myself and left. I saw her in the building every now and then, but she kept a polite distance, and didn't speak to me again except to say hi.

On Saturday, the day of my first date in what seemed like forever, she was at the pool again while I did my laps. I was so relieved all of a sudden. Maybe I needed to talk to someone? Just tell a friend that *oh my god I'm going on a date with this really cute guy?* Was that a legitimate reason to break the code of neighborly conduct we'd set?

I swam toward Matilda. She was wearing a shiny green bikini, very mermaid-like. I waved to her. "Hi," I said.

Matilda nodded and sort of wiggled her hips, making herself comfortable on the chair. "Hey, Iris."

"Hi." God, I should have prepared a script. I wasn't used to making friends anymore.

She frowned. "Anything wrong? Is anyone in the building giving you shit? Someone bothering you?"

I laughed. "No. I'm sorry. I just wanted to say hi, so now I did. Twice. I'm so bad at this. Why, what are you going to do about it?"

"If someone were bothering you? I'll give them a piece of my mind."

"Oh. Thanks. But so far, no one."

"Good. Do you avoid the internet now?"

"What?"

"After what happened to you."

That first time, Matilda had been refreshingly direct too, but still polite. This was someone I needed in my life, perhaps. I'd only ever talked about this with my therapist, but I actually *didn't* avoid the internet. I knew when to look away, sure, but I kept tabs on the activity that the video had online. I had Google alerts for my name. It took a lot of discipline for me to stop looking at it, but they were all still there.

"No," I said. "Why?"

"Interesting," she replied. "I'm serious. If anyone gives you a dirty look and you don't feel safe living here anymore, you tell me, okay?"

How could I say no to that? "Sure."

"If you can figure out some search words based on the short conversation we've had, and what I've told you, then great. You'll know that I have my own drama, and I mean what I said. I'd bitchslap anyone who gives you a hard time. You've been living here more than a year now, right? So how do you like it so far?"

"NV Park? It's cool. I like the buildings. And no one has bothered me about that thing."

"Are you seeing anyone?"

She headed straight for her targets, didn't she? I didn't even have to steer her in the direction I needed her to. "Maybe. Oh god. I may have started to talk to you right now because I wanted to tell someone how nervous I am about it."

"That's great," Matilda said, nodding her approval. "That's awesome. Don't be nervous. It's not the same guy in the video with you?"

"Oh, it's not."

"Moving on is the best thing. Does he live in NV Park? It's okay if you don't tell me, but I know all kinds of shit about residents here. You might want it."

"I'm not sure I'm ready for that."

"Honey," Matilda said, stretching and smiling. "I've been waiting for you to be friendly about anything. I'll be as useful or as useless to you as you like."

"He's the guy in 9J," I said. "That's all I'll say for now."

"Oh. Tower 3?"

"Yeah."

"Hmm."

"Is that good or bad? No, you know what? Don't say anything." 9J was off the grid for a reason, and I needed to respect that. I needed to be the person I wished other people were, about my own privacy.

Matilda had a pair of sunglasses resting on her flat belly, and she toyed with it for a bit. "Fine, no dirt. But do you want us to be friends now?"

"Of course. I didn't mean to be—"

"No worries, Iris. I have a Saturday afternoon snack date with some friends. You want to join us later?"

"I can't today, I'm sorry."

"Next week?"

A date, and friends, all of a sudden. "Okay," I said, trying to hide how overwhelmed I felt. Because I shouldn't have been. New Normal. Ready for this. "I need new friends. Are they like you?"

Matilda laughed. "No and yes. I'll let you find out for yourself when you meet them. We usually pick a restaurant across the street. Will just let you know when we've decided."

"Sure, great. I like the places over there. I enjoy living here."

"I know. It's why I came back, as soon as I could. I wanted to claim this back."

It was the kind of thing someone said when they wanted you to ask them about it, and I was going to, but my phone began to ring.

"Sorry," I said, wading to the other side of the shallow end to pick up my phone from its spot on top of my small folded pile of clothes and a towel.

It was my brother. Shit.

"Liam," I said, even though the number that flashed was the home landline.

"You should come on Sunday." True enough it was him; it wouldn't have been anyone else.

Liam's voice reminded me of playtime ending. He was just a year older than me but he was always first back inside from the backyard. *Come on, Iris,* was always the thing I heard, right before the house swallowed me up. "I don't think so."

"You remember what day it is, right?"

"It's Saturday."

"You can do better than that."

I sighed. "It's your birthday."

"Jackpot."

"Technically, it was your birthday two days ago."

"Right, and I'm not going to mention how annoying it is that you didn't show up to my wine bar soiree."

Because I didn't particularly like his "wine bar" friends. "You're very good at not mentioning stuff."

"I'm very talented."

"Can't you come over here and I'll take you out to dinner? There are a gazillion restaurants here you haven't tried."

"It's my birthday and I get to tell you where to go, Little Flower."

"That's not how it works. And never call me that again."

"Come to the house at one."

"No."

"Come at two."

"No."

"Fine. Come at three, come in through the back, and it'll be you and me. In the backyard. Just us."

"Just us?"

"Yes, only the misfits."

Oh, but he really wasn't that. Liam may have gotten through most of his adult life facing a different kind of struggle from mine, but I wouldn't have labeled him a misfit. He happened to be successful, grounded, stubbornly affectionate.

"You're not a misfit."

"The token gay in this family gets to call himself whatever he wants."

"Just us?" I asked, relenting.

"Just us and caramel crunch cake."

"Maybe." I didn't say *yes*. I hadn't been back at home for Sunday lunch in a long time. But a Liam-birthday Sunday Lunch was the same kind of nerve-wracking experience, times twenty, especially after The Incident.

Despite my waffling, he reacted as if I'd said yes. "Happy birthday to me," Liam practically cooed. "I love you."

FOUR

"At all? Nothing?"

"There's bottled pesto in aisle twelve, ma'am."

Well yeah, but that wasn't the point! I didn't need premade pesto in a jar. I needed fresh basil, which the grocery store at the NV Park complex always had.

"I'm sorry," the lady stocking the vegetables told me. "There was a new delivery this morning, but it's all out by now."

Because everyone else in the neighborhood just decided to stay in on a Saturday and make their own pesto? How much basil did a person need? And today of all days? Didn't they realize how important this day was to me?

"Arugula?" Grocery Lady said.

"*No,*" I replied, as whiny as my thoughts. "It won't taste the same. I can't believe this is happening. There's basil on this shelf every day, when I don't need it."

So it had come to this—I was close to throwing a tantrum at the fresh produce section, to a person who probably had better things to worry about than my self-confidence. *Get a grip, woman!* But that was precisely it, I was hanging on to this dish because it was familiar. For all the stuff I had to let go of, some things I clung to because they helped me cope, kept some part of me intact. Pesto linguini and buttered rolls—that was me. I needed it.

God, no basil. What else did I have? Eggplant parmigiana...but that needed basil. The chicken stew I made whenever I got sick...but that needed a gazillion other vegetables and would look like I was trying too hard for 9J. Fish? Could I do something with fish?

"Spinach?" Grocery Lady added, and I had to love her concern. "But really, ma'am, the bottled pesto should be okay."

It wouldn't be, because those were too salty all the time, and I had a thing against that. The point was that I was in control, if I had the ingredients and made my own dish. After The Incident, couldn't I make the choice how much salt went into my food? Couldn't I have even that?

"Thank you," I told her. "I guess I need to do something else."

"...AND that's how we ended up with this."

"Well, it's very good pizza."

"I know, right?"

You would think that the nighttime and the darkness that came with it would make those eyes of his less conspicuous, but no, it was like they took the artificial light from the buildings around us and sucked them in, so they'd be bluer, brighter, and I'd have a tougher time trying not to stupidly stare. The hair was away from his face again, and it was insane how I just then realized how hair framed a face. His eyes were the center of everything. It was a clear face too—

not the stubbly kind, had never seen him with any phase of beard yet. Maybe he was one of those guys? Bradley had needed to shave every day.

Needs that were neglected for some time stirred up inside.

Seriously. I told my needs. *You barely know the guy.*

...But he doesn't know you either, my needs seemed to be saying back. *Isn't it better that way?*

"...I wouldn't have chosen this cheese," he was saying.

He was referring to the cop-out pizza I'd ordered, from the place across the street that let us choose our own toppings from a selection that included melons, gorgonzola, and pork floss. After assuring Grocery Lady that I was not on the verge of a breakdown, I threw out all attempts at a homemade meal and dropped by the pizza place.

But I chose the toppings, because *control.* There might be melon, gorgonzola, and pork floss in this pizza. I was on autopilot at that point, with less than an hour to go before I had to pick him up, and I was all out of ideas. I had wanted to show up with my comfort dish, best foot forward, and instead showed up with Frankenpizza.

9J could hate it, whatever. Other people had rejected me for worse.

"...but it works," he concluded. "Shit, I'm missing out. Did you know this worked?"

"God, I didn't," I said. "I had a bad afternoon and kind of just pointed at things at random. You're sure you're okay with it?"

"It's growing on me."

"Maybe they have a special sauce that makes sure all the toppings come together."

He was chewing, considering it. "I don't know. Without the melon it would be different."

"I never thought I'd say that my pizza needed more melon."

"No sauce is ever going to fix that." He reached for the bottle of root beer and refilled his paper cup, then mine.

Obviously this was a classy first-date dinner. The view of the Tower 3 pool at night made up for it. I checked if anyone had reserved the poolside for guests, because other residents did that sometimes, and was assured that it was clear. So that Saturday evening on the seventh floor pool and common area, it was just 9J and me and our strange little pizza on the picnic table. We could see out into the main NV Park residential and business complex, where we were sitting. A cluster of buildings, offices lit up for the night shift, bright signs of open restaurants and shops below. And people, lots of people.

I saw that he was looking down at them as well.

"What do you do, 9J?" I asked.

His eyes shifted to me, his smile a bit sheepish. "I am... unemployed right now. But I have a degree in chemical engineering."

"You could have started with the engineering."

"I know, but you should probably know it anyway."

"Bad job market?"

"Kind of," he said. "I was expected to go into the formulation side of the family business, but that didn't pan out."

"Oh? Why?"

His smile turned up, and now it was a little bit naughty boy again. "Because I can't stand them."

"Ooh. Interesting. Did you quit with drama?"

"Yes, there was some of that."

"And you're a runaway? Are you hiding here in NV Park, trying to figure out what to do next with your life?"

"Something like that."

No phone, recent runaway, wouldn't tell me his name. Bad News with a scoop of Watch Out topped with a What Are You Even Thinking. I wondered if he was a criminal, like an actual fugitive, but the building admins would have known who he was somehow, and they wouldn't have let him lease an apartment.

Unless he forged papers? Bribed authorities? Was on the run from *justice?* But that was too complicated.

Someone suggested that I legally change my name, by the way. It was advice that was meant to be helpful, and maybe it was reasonable, because I got Google alerts with my name daily and they weren't good employment references at all. But coming from a relative whose name I shared, it felt like a stab to the heart.

9J's drama couldn't have been too different from mine. The way he carried himself, how *polished* he looked...maybe he really was just avoiding an overbearing family.

Don't judge, I told myself. "I think it's a club," I told him. "Runaways hiding in this apartment complex."

"Runaways with money."

I shrugged. "Some of us go to a job every day and that's how we get new money."

He grinned at the dig, not that I had any evidence he was filthy rich. He wasn't exactly denying it either. What did you run away from, 9J? I was curious, but felt like this was a reciprocity kind of thing—if he gave me a detail, I'd have to give him one of mine. I wasn't sure how much I was ready to share.

"So," I said, "Do you get asked about your eyes a lot?"

"I don't get asked about it at all," he said. "Because people don't ask. They just—call it out."

"What?"

"Blue Eyes. You know what some people from grade school continue to call me, to this day?"

I laughed. "Blue?"

"That's right."

"Kids should be more imaginative than that."

"They went for the obvious, of course. Blue, Uncle Sam, Contacts."

"Why would they even make fun of you? You look like you could punch them in the face." I said that without thinking, and now he knew I'd been checking out his firm forearms way more than I should have.

"Well, I was thinner," he said. Exactly what did he mean by thin anyway? That chest and shoulders, those arms, they were glorious. "And shorter."

I shook my head. "Kids don't know what they're saying, do they? Most of the time. It's too easy to point out what's different. I'm assuming they did that because you were the only blue-eyed boy in class?"

He nodded. "I got used to it. It was safer, actually."

"Safer?"

"I hated it, until I saw how they made fun of people for what they did."

"I'm sorry—like how?"

"Like when they made fun of the guy who tripped during the track meet. Or the guy who came back from the spelling bee in third place because he missed a word."

"What did they call them?"

"I'm trying not to remember."

"People can be..." Cruel? Awful? Yes they could be, even kids. I didn't want to make this about The Incident, as so many things already were.

"Dumb," 9J said, shrugging. "But that's typical stuff kids do, right? Make fun of those who try things. If that had happened to me, I wouldn't have even gone out there. So it was safer, that they made fun of something I already had. At least I already had a shitty nickname, and they couldn't keep me from anything worth doing."

"What did you end up doing?"

"What?"

"The thing, that they would have made fun of you for. What did you end up doing?"

He paused. "Nothing that those grade school bullies would have known about."

"'Blue' is not such a bad thing to be known for."

"Oh it isn't," he quickly added. "Feel free to call me Blue as much as you want. If that's what you're into. What are you into, 9M?"

"Pizza."

"The strange but good kind. What else? What do you do?"

Throughout dinner he had been remarkably decent, even based on my new and expanded need for personal space. He stayed a respectable distance from me, didn't touch me inappropriately, held his head in that way that would have been seen as shy, if he had less of a presence. I may have spent too much time worrying about identifying pervs, forgetting how it was to act around a decent guy.

How did this go again?

"Scholarship services," I said. "Is the boring way to describe what I do."

"Is there a sexy way to describe it?"

I stifled a laugh. "I help women get money to study science and math, if they want to."

"See, that sounds like a real job. A really awesome one."

"Unemployed Chemical Engineer is not?"

"Unfortunately. Do you like what you do?"

"I like it," I said. "I mean, I can't hate it. It's great what they're doing."

"The pay any good?"

"Just enough to let me make the rent and a little extra. But I don't need a lot of things."

"I don't have a lot of things either. Good policy to have."

"That's what another runaway would say. Not so easy to quit a family business, I guess?"

There was a flicker of sadness in those eyes, whenever something we said swung a certain way. I knew what it was because it was probably the same thing in mine. Shit, why didn't we just meet at a bar or something? We could have at least been talking about how stupid it was, meeting at a bar, instead of this. Instead of ourselves.

"Oh for some people it is," he said, exhaling, the sentence feeling loaded. "But not me. Something else was expected from me. I'm the good one."

"Good is so overrated," I teased. "You never know what people are thinking. Or doing. Or doing when they think you're not looking."

I meant that to be light and fluffy, but the sadness showed up in his eyes and mine too, and damn it. Talking in riddles on the first date was difficult. But then 9J snapped out of it first.

"You know what I do when I think no one's looking?" he asked.

"Sit-ups on the roof?"

"No." He checked the time on his phone, then tilted his head toward the elevators in the hallway. "Come on."

FIVE

NV Park Tower 2 had a slightly different color scheme; shades of blue and teal where our tower was reddish brown. I'd probably only crossed over to the tower next door to pick something up from the admin office there, and never made it up to the eighth floor recreational area. The common areas were all a little different, probably to target a different kind of demographic of residents. Tower 1 had gardens and "meditation areas," Tower 3 had a big gym and workout-ready pool. Tower 2 had pool tables and a party area with what could pass for a bar.

Not that people were using it on Saturday nights to party hard—it was empty and dark, pretty much, when we got there.

"This looks like the saddest club I've ever seen," I told him.

"Why are you whispering?"

"I don't know. Is it okay that we're here at this hour?"

"Of course it is."

The common areas in the different towers were open-air, and the lights were all shut. 9J headed over in the direction of the wall and flipped a switch. Light came on in one quadrant of the space, illuminating an unused pool table.

Unused only in a manner of speaking, because nearly the entire surface of it was occupied by lots, and lots, and *lots* of jigsaw puzzle pieces. Separate pieces, scattered haphazardly around a small section of completed puzzle, which was a portion barely larger than an A4 size paper.

"What is this?"

"I don't know."

"I mean I know it's a puzzle, but why is it so large? What's it supposed to look like?"

9J went right for a small pile of pieces and picked it up, showing me an orange-colored one. "That's what I meant; I don't know what it's supposed to look like. The guards told me that a tenant with a hobbyist kid left it here, and then gave up on it. No one was using the pool table anyway, and they noticed that residents were dropping by and giving it a shot, so they never threw it out."

The piece he showed me didn't look like anything. The rest of those in the pile, all various shades of orange, didn't make sense to me either. Then I noticed the other small piles, grouped by similar colors, and the others seemed prominently brown, and black, and gray.

"I suspect," 9J added, "that it's a photo of the sky at sunset. So most of the puzzle will be based on a gradient background that's probably a lot of red and orange and that's why we've got all these variations on the same color."

"You're the one grouping the same-color pieces?"

"Well yeah. Makes sense to do it that way, without a reference photo."

"Holy crap." There were a *lot* of pieces, if I hadn't stressed that enough. The puzzle, when completed, would probably take up most of the pool table. "So no one else in the building has used the pool table since then?"

9J tested the piece he was holding against the portion of puzzle. No, didn't fit. "It's a thing, in this tower. The guards see people keep coming back to try to put a piece in."

"Through CCTV?"

"Yeah. Apparently some people take their friends and look at this monstrosity."

"Or their dates," I said.

His eyebrow sort of quirked there. "This too strange for you?"

"So you actually come over here to do this? How often?"

"A couple times a week. And only if there's no one else here. It's very relaxing, have to admit."

Oh, I understood. I could imagine how this kind of thing could take over your brain for however much time you gave it. The satisfaction finding that one piece that fit in the right space. In the past two years I'd been told to take up everything from yoga to pottery to sword-fighting, anything to get my mind off myself. Instead I just went on as usual, but in private.

"Are you really into this?" I asked him, my fingers tracing the curves on a reddish piece. "Or is it because you get to kill time without anyone bothering you?"

"I have other hobbies. Social ones."

"Like what?"

"I'm on the Saturday football team. That's where I came from, earlier."

"Oh, do you play on the open field outside?"

"Yeah we do."

"That's very well-adjusted of you then."

"But yes," he said, "I come up here when I don't feel

like talking to anyone. And that's a lot more than usual, lately. You probably understand why."

"Of course I do." Because we were runaways.

That shared look again. So strongly I wished that I could know, for sure, if he really understood. My mind flashed forward to a possible future of me finding out that he had played me, pretended not to have recognized me, got me into bed after two dates and a sob story, lost interest after he'd had the real thing and preferred the video version. Video version Iris had a smaller waist, tighter abs. She was regularly working out though she didn't like it. Her boyfriend at the time liked that she worked out and regularly complimented the results.

"9M," and he let that trail off, as he tested the piece against another part of the puzzle, and grunted with satisfaction when the piece slid in and locked. It was a good sound. "Do you really want to do this?"

"Do I really want to spend the rest of the night putting this puzzle together? Seems impossible. So no."

"No one wants to do that all night. I mean, this." Him and me, as his finger dutifully began pointing. "No names? No specifics?"

Why not? It wasn't that much more awkward or difficult than a real first date with someone who knew my name.

Or he really needed to talk to someone too.

"I don't have the best references," I said. "You might not like what you find out."

"I'd say the same about myself."

"Yeah, but you'll have your career back, once you find a job. You have football friends. My situation is different, I'm sure."

"Are you married?"

Haha. I probably would have been, by now, had The Incident not happened. "No. Are you?"

"No. Is there a warrant for your arrest or something?"

"No. You?"

"No. Shit, this is so strange. You're beautiful, and I've noticed you around the building for some time now. I've been living here a year."

"What? And you never said anything until the elevator?"

9J threw his hands up, frustrated at something. "I'm a mess. I've been trying not to make myself into someone's problem."

"I can bet you big money we both don't have that I'm a bigger mess than you."

"Don't dare me."

"Yeah, like you scare me. You can't even save yourself in a stalled elevator."

"Not fair."

"Well, that's practically all I know about you."

"Don't dare me."

"You already said that."

He didn't have to say it a third time because by then his mouth was on mine, and we were kissing.

I MISSED KISSING.

Oh god, I missed it. I'd always enjoyed it, all different ways it could be done, lips and tongues and mouths, sweet, urgent, messy, angry, all of it. I loved how vulnerable it made me, how powerful too. What I could find out from the person from the kiss itself, things that he'd never say. Or hadn't said yet.

It was my idea to go to 9M, my place. After the breakup with Bradley, and when I came to accept that I would be kissing someone else eventually, I told myself that it had to be on my terms. It would have been against my instincts to invite a new guy into my home on what was essentially a first date, but this guy already knew where I lived.

And I knew I had no cameras around.

We fell onto the couch. No, I pushed him down there and leaped right on top of him. Kissing, I told myself, just kissing. His lips were strong, I remembered thinking, holding up well against my attack, because it felt to me like I was pushing so hard. He groaned, and pulled me closer, tongue tasting mine. It was like he missed kissing too.

His skin was warm. *Lick it. Lick him,* the thought came quickly, and I did, from his chin down to his throat, nibbling the skin there. He made a sound; no words, but the hand on my hip pulled me in and ground me against a seriously hard erection.

Maybe he missed something else also?

I should tell him. That I wasn't intending to have sex with someone whose name I didn't even know, regardless of how much I missed it. But instead of saying words, I made sounds too, and pushed another kiss deep into his mouth.

He responded to that just the way I wanted him to—with surprise, then acceptance, then retaliation. He gave back as much as he got; my tongue got a workout. This guy was going to be so good, I could tell.

If we could get past the point when I'd tell him he could watch me have sex with someone else, online.

When was the right time to tell someone? Was I expected to mention it when I accepted his dinner invite? If he didn't already know, was he supposed to hear it from me?

One of Janine's main messages of comfort to me was

that the world of people who watched sex videos *was not the entire world*. Sure, they were millions upon millions of people, but they were not the world, and I could live my entire life never having to meet any of those people.

Those millions of people.

But there was a greater circle that surrounded that, of people who probably wouldn't watch, but would judge. Would care. Would get the hell out of this couch before sticking more of his tongue down my throat.

What did 9J deserve to know?

It's none of his business, Janine had said. *You'll find it best to move on from people who will make you feel like shit because of what happened. It wasn't your fault.*

That was comforting and decent-human-being of her, but here's the thing: *I* would want to know.

I'd asked Bradley a bunch of questions when we became serious. Who had he done this with? Was I going to be at risk for something? Was someone going to be coming at me for revenge? And he and I both, we gave our answers, revealed our cards.

Shit. 9J was so good-looking, and great at kissing. I couldn't just keep all of this from him.

"We won't, you know," I said, tearing my mouth from his.

He blinked and tried to focus. "Won't what?"

"Have sex right now. Not when we don't even know each other."

"Oh, that." He shook his head a little, waking himself up. "Of course. I totally understand."

"I'm glad you do." This conversation didn't change how I was still straddling him, still touching the skin of his throat with my fingers. But maybe I didn't want to let go just yet.

Knowing that there was a ninety percent chance that I was going to get dumped.

"Or we could just tell each other our names now," he said.

"So we can feel better about hooking up with a stranger?"

"With a neighbor. You're hooking up with a neighbor, not a stranger."

"If it were that easy then why haven't you told me yours yet?"

He sighed, pressing his lips against my neck. "Shit."

"I understand."

"I should explain," he said, looking back up at me, putting those eyes in my view again. "I should."

"Okay."

"I didn't kill anyone. I'm not a criminal. I'm not married, or a drug dealer. I don't have a sexually-transmitted infection or anything."

Well, neither did I. "You're just an unemployed chemical engineer."

"Well, not just." Whatever it was, he had a hard time composing his next sentence.

"Is it something I'll find out about you if I Google your name?"

He nodded. "Yes."

That already filled in half the blanks. "That's funny. Me too."

"So you seriously don't know who I am? You don't know what I'm talking about?"

"You mean what you're *not* talking about. No, I don't. You're kind of hyping it up like it's this wicked giant thing though."

"It's a big deal *to me*. I don't want anyone to have to

worry about it." Then it dawned on him, what was happening here. "That's your thing too?"

"Kind of. You don't recognize me either, do you?"

He shook his head. "I don't. But it can't be that bad."

"If it weren't *that bad* we'd be doing something else right now. We're obviously not over it, whatever our things are."

"Damn it." Still, he wasn't letting go. I felt his hands caressing my shoulder blades, cupping them, cradling them. "If it's worth anything, I think you're hot, and I enjoyed talking to you."

"Past tense?"

"I understand if you never want to see me again, once you find out."

"We live on the same floor."

"I'm going to be easy to avoid," he said, with sad blue eyes. "I make it easy for people to do that."

I kissed him again. We kissed like it was goodbye, pulled and strained against clothing that never came off. We kissed for a long time, more than an hour I'm sure, and then it was him who sighed a real goodbye and headed to my door, toward his own cave around the corner.

"Gio Mella," he said.

"Iris Len-Larioca," I said.

He smiled. "Good night, Iris."

"Good night, Gio."

WHY DID I have to be the kind of person who liked looking up stuff? And reading it? And clicking more, and reading more, until I knew too much? You'd think that I would have thrown my laptop away. But it actually provided reassurance, seeing how much less The Incident was being talked about, in the weeks and months that followed.

When I got to bed I lay there, thinking about 9J—Gio's name. Gio Mella. It was vaguely familiar, but I wouldn't win any quizzes on naming celebrities or famous people anyway. I only knew that it wasn't the last name of any of my friends, relatives, anyone I worked with. I also wondered how it was spelled, because it probably would have been on a sign or a building somewhere? Since there seemed to be a prominent family business and all.

Gio, though. So that was his name. I didn't even know what I was expecting.

You can do it. I mean, he expects you to.

So I did the thing, on Google.

gio mella scandal

Which was what you did, if you needed to know that thing that the guy you just met was hiding from.

SIX

"Why do you look like shit? You can't even be bothered to look decent on my birthday."

"Shut up, Liam." My voice probably sounded like a frog's, but it was appropriately affectionate, I hoped. Liam would have understood; we'd been sarcastically affectionate for most of our lives. "Happy birthday."

At least, I hoped he understood. But when I lowered my sunglasses as I gave him a kiss on the cheek, and immediately my eyes began to water from the slight exposure to the afternoon, I wondered if I did lower the bar this time around.

I didn't get much sleep.

He looked happy, though, which was what mattered. Liam was single right now, and I wasn't sure if he'd be in a "mood" on his birthday. Leave it to my brother though to be consistently the life of his own party, no matter what was happening in his life.

When I saw what he had set up for me, the sunglasses came back on to keep him from seeing the tears welling up. He'd pulled out the plastic table from the utility room and set it for two. It was a freaking tea party—pot of tea, two dainty matching cups, caramel crunch cake.

"So how was your party, party boy?" I asked.

"Oh, you know. The same."

"It can't be. Twenty-five, right? You always said it would be a great one."

"Oh, you mean the wine bar party, the real one that you missed? With kids our age and not our aging relatives and their amigas? Of course that was the best. I greeted my mid-twenties with a bang."

"God," I said, taking the plastic chair that I assumed was mine. "I sure hope you meant the good kind of bang."

He grabbed my hand, forcing it into a high-five with his. "Why yes, sister. The good kind of bang."

"Safe?"

"No other way." He scooted his chair closer to mine. "Your concern is always appreciated."

And then we were quiet. Liam and I were close, and never had trouble talking, even when the worst was happening around us. That was one of the things I had taken as truth, and never tested. Today, I was here at home for the first time in a long time because of him, but it wasn't only *him* here. There was a lot to be processed.

This chair. That table. The backyard, the smell of dirt and grass. That door that led to the kitchen, and to the dining room. Those voices, the familiar tones of Sunday afternoon *merienda* conversation.

It wasn't as scary as I was making it out to be. Right?

"Hey." Liam snapped a finger in front of me. "Anything new with you?"

Oh, how to even talk about it. My brother was often concerned for me, and the past few times he'd asked "anything new?" I'd nothing to add. I was fine, nothing's new, good bye and see you next time. We tolerated this for months because there was no way to talk about what was better. Maybe he hoped that I'd say something good, because it meant life had moved on beyond two years ago.

What could I tell him now? Where would I even begin?

The doors to the backyard slid open, and some of the voices from inside came out, in their fleshy bodies too. See, this shouldn't have been a problem. I'd prepared myself mentally for this moment, for being at home, and seeing certain people. I'd steeled my guts for this, knowing I had to at some point, and Liam's birthday was a good time to start.

Still, it felt like my blood ran cold.

"Oh my god," my mother said, clearly shocked. "Iris, I didn't know you were coming."

"Oh my god, hija," my dad's older sister, Tita Ara, said at the same time. "Were you here the whole time?"

"I just arrived," I told her.

"...because Liam, I told you I'd be inviting Councilor Kit. And Brother Julian. And we were taking so many photos..."

And the worst thing in the world would be if I were accidentally in a photo with them. In my own house.

Liam cleared his throat. "No, Tita, Mom, you know I never invite the cool guests into the house with the old people. Your visitors are safe from us."

Tita Ara was not a fool. In fact she was the very definition of "not a fool," at least for me, and she had an influence over my mother and this house. Our house was hers, our parties hers, my shame hers. "This isn't a joke, Liam," she said. "Will there be trouble?"

"None at all," I said, standing up. "I came over to greet Liam. And I've done that. I'll go now."

"I didn't realize..." My mother was stuck in the world

from ninety seconds ago, still struggling to come up with the proper thing to say. "Iris, you should at least say hello to your dad..."

Well, how could I even do that? After this awkwardness fest. I'd already said I was going, so I did that, standing up and backing away. I knew no one would stop me—the one thing they always let me do, throughout this mess, was walk away.

And so I walked, in my white tennis shoes, sunglasses my only disguise. I let myself out the white gate, but took the alley that led to the back street, and then didn't stop until I made it out to the main road, where I could hail a cab.

My phone was ringing. It was vibrating in my little bag, but I ignored it for as long as I could, answering only when it started up again.

"Come back, Iris," Liam said.

"No," I told my brother. "I can't believe that all happened, again."

"I'm sorry. I didn't think—it's my birthday, damn it. I thought they'd be better."

"Yeah well, that sucks, because it's not me. It's them. I love you but you won't ever put me in that position again, okay?"

"I'm really sorry. Let me make it up to you."

"There's nothing you can do."

"At least let me drive you back?"

"I'm already in a cab." That was a lie, clearly. "I'll see you around."

Well, shit. There went that possibility of normal.

I told myself that I wouldn't resort to alcohol to numb myself, when these things happened. Numbing led to bad decisions, and I couldn't afford a grander fuckup than what was already there. The Incident had led me to lose not only most of my family but also my closest friends so I had very few options for venting and relief.

I had Janine, sure, but calling Janine on a Sunday? That was serious. That was dignifying this as a major thing, and I wanted it downgraded, demoted, crushed into the ground.

So when the cab let me out at NV Park, I bought a bottled water and walked. And walked and walked. Walked around the complex, past the open field where 9J—Gio apparently played football on Saturdays. Past the restaurants where I bought my meals. Past the grocery store that would probably have basil right now, because I didn't need it. Past the office buildings, the pet park, the jogging trail, around and around until I had gone around four times or more, and the sun was setting.

Sometimes I did this, when things even if only in my head, went a little crazy. The endorphins lifted my mood, the silence of the walk cleared my head, the bright and busy scenery was no longer scary but a crowd I could hide in.

Sometimes it worked, and by the end of the journey I was less angry, felt less of a victim. Or maybe it was the body chemistry telling me to go on another day, because the world, yes, had more things in it than the things and people I didn't like.

By the time I made it back to my tower, I had given a few things a *lot* of thought.

I left a message for Matilda at the lobby receptionist's desk.

And then I slipped a note underneath Gio Mella's door.

I don't care, it said. *I hope you don't too.*

Iris Len-Larioca, 9M.

SEVEN

So I realized this, after hours of searching, reading, and watching—my neighbor had his own brush with unexpected fame and shame. Gio Mella was internet-famous for the wrong reasons, for nine days.

That was about the length of time from the first gossip blog post about him (a teaser-type blind item, not naming names), to the post naming names, to the subsequent photos, the articles reacting to it, the blog posts reacting to the articles, the mainstream news media and television entertainment news picking up the "incident."

The last significant coverage of it was an interview with Leslie Tracy Rivera, apparently a young actress, and she spent the ten minutes of air time with teary eyes and a creased forehead. The creased forehead of judgment.

Let's back up for a bit, because I had to. I didn't even know who she was, and why this was at all significant. But the answers of the internet were soon mine:

Leslie Tracy Rivera was a former child actress with one hit movie credit. Now in her early twenties, she'd resurfaced on television with a few minor roles in afternoon soaps. The few features on her (pre-Incident), made it seem like it wasn't working out all that well—she was pretty, sure, but they had no shortage of "pretty," "sweet," and "perfect smile" in that industry.

Young actress Leslie Tracy Rivera is "fine" with taking it slow

The article was from several years ago. Yes, she had a boyfriend now, it said. Yes, he wasn't from the business. *Does this mean you're ready for more mature roles? What about your young fans?*

"Having a boyfriend doesn't have to mean I'm no longer a role model," Leslie says. "Gio is one of the good guys. He's willing to wait until marriage, and I love him for it."

When I read that I was over an hour into this web crawl, and sleepy, and compulsively clicking everything against my better judgment. I should have been a zombie and reacted to this as ambivalently as the undead would, but I couldn't. My stomach turned, and the map of how this scandal unfolded formed in my mind.

Leslie Tracy Rivera celebrates new movie with supportive boyfriend Gio Mella

True love waits? Celeb couples who are counting down to marriage

Breakup rumors untrue: Leslie Tracy Rivera insists boyfriend "not like that"

Good girl gone bad? Former child star spotted in clubs

Leslie Tracy Rivera spends birthday at orphanage: "This is the real me"

Sadly, there was nothing about the fact that he had a chemical engineering degree, or that he had an actual life apart from being this girl's "supportive boyfriend." Not that the news should have been filled with the lives and drama of our chemical engineers, but anyway.

When you sorted the actual news items by date, earliest first, they came at you as slowly or as quickly as you want it. Life unfolding. A trainwreck you can slow down or speed up.

Then last year, his Incident. It was Leslie's twenty-second birthday party, in the family home; she may have skipped the birthday do-gooding that year, and then would later come to regret it. She looked happy in the photos at the birthday itself. Then, a few days later, a barrage of new information, and comments that were horrible but not far from the truth.

Does Birthday Girl know what happened at her party?
Good Guy Boyfriend sick of waiting
Photo: Good Guy Boyfriend and Birthday Girl's SISTER
New Photo: Good Guy Boyfriend and Birthday Girl's FRIEND
"Good Guy Boyfriend" not waiting — Birthday Girl should dump him now!
Date a guy who tells the TRUTH. #TeamBirthdayGirl

I clicked on the posts with photos. I knew I shouldn't have—the many times I'd wished that people would give me the courtesy of thinking of me as a PERSON and not a SEXUAL PLAYTHING were pushed back by my own hideous curiosity. I wanted to see what had ruined him.

Photos, though. Not video. That was Gio all right, or someone who looked a lot like him. Shirt off. A beautiful girl's long hair tangled around his fingers, her lips fused to his. If this was Leslie Tracy Rivera's sister, I'd take the internet's word for it.

Then, the friend. It was another photo, and they weren't kissing, but this girl with shorter hair was stripped down her bra and was straddling him. It was still him, yes, and the girl's lipstick was smeared.

The comment section had the usual trash of humanity: People calling Leslie's sister and Leslie's friend "whores." How long has this been going on. Of course he couldn't wait, he's a man. Gio Mella was a "manwhore." Key words, all of them, instantly familiar because the same words popped up in the comment threads about me.

People needed a better attitude. Or a damn thesaurus.

Leslie gave a teary interview on TV, where she expressed outrage at these photos, but did not "stand by her man." She broke up with him, condemned his filthy acts, and took on a starring role in a mini-series as a nun. By the next day the mentions tapered off, displaced in the internet chaos by some other thing.

How could I have missed this? What was I busy with, that nine days of someone else's scandal would fly over my head? Was I in the middle of breaking up with Bradley? Did I lose my broadband connection?

Would this have been the kind of thing that got my interest, if I'd been interested? Maybe not. None of my friends would have brought it up either.

Nine days. And then Gio Mella, youngest son of the owners of Bella Mariel Cosmetics, disappeared from the internet. Apparently also disconnected himself from it, and decided to live off-the-grid in NV Park, as an unemployed chemical engineer.

Down the hall from me.

Funny how life turned out, sometimes.

TUESDAY CAME, and no word from Gio.

I guessed that he cared after all. It felt like my first major rejection after *my* Incident. Maybe two years was too soon? Because the internet may have stopped caring about you, but the fact that it happened at all—

Well.

Shit.

Sigh.

So by Tuesday night, as I dragged my rejected moody self all the way home, I was going through the stages. Had I accepted that this happened to me? Well, no. But apparently, I was now a beggar who couldn't be choosy. I had put myself at the mercy of people's judgment, and I had to expect that they'd be unkind.

At least the message for Matilda had a better response. We were meeting for lunch that weekend. *"I'll introduce you to my friends,"* she'd said, quickly adding that I shouldn't at all freak out. *"They're a good bunch."*

How dumb do you feel right now, Iris Len-Larioca?

Damn it, I'd told him who I was. That was enough time to find whatever he needed to see, and the silence sounded a lot like judgment. And it wasn't like he was all clean himself.

And...didn't I deserve to get a rejection to my face? He knew where he could find me. No note, even? Not enough paper to say "It's not you, it's me"?

I wanted to say something. I didn't get to say, too often, to people's faces what hypocrites they were, and I was itching for that release.

I'll do that. Give him a piece of my mind.

You can reject me, fine, but don't just avoid me like I'm supposed to accept that what happened to me was the worst thing.

I didn't kill anyone. I didn't steal money. I don't deserve to be treated worse than you do common criminals.

You know what—you're worse than me!

It was possible that my anger was jumbling people and timelines in my head. But helpless anger was what I had, and it was worse at settling down than a two-year-old child. Not proud of it, but all the same, I charged out of my apartment near midnight, and headed right for his. And banged on his door loud enough to wake the neighbors.

No answer.

Was he asleep?

The sane thing to do was to abort the mission and head back to home base, but nooooo. The bitter words needed escape, and they fueled my trip down the elevator to the lobby, across to the other tower, and then back up to Tower 2's recreational area, where, just as I thought, Gio was working on the giant puzzle.

You really shouldn't date your neighbors, if you want to be left alone.

Maybe you shouldn't make out with your neighbors and then ditch them.

Maybe you should—

"Look," I said, the words coming out, struggling but sounding quite possibly human. "I know that decent people probably don't want anything to do with me. I've spent the past two years accepting it. I'm not going to be surprised if you think it's too much for you, but I want, no I deserve to be told to my face that I'm going to be dumped, like anyone else who's getting dumped—"

Gio was holding several puzzle pieces and he dropped them, right on top of piles where they didn't belong, and circled around the pool table to get closer to me. The kiss he placed on my mouth was unexpected, because it was exactly the opposite of what my whole rant was about.

Wait. We're kissing. Oh.

He didn't let up until I relaxed and kissed him back.

The bitter words didn't go away. They sort of backed up though, recognizing that they weren't meant for this guy. This guy wasn't one of those people. This guy was gently nibbling at my lower lip, then teasing me with the tip of his tongue.

Okay then.

"Iris," he said, when he pulled back. "I'm sorry. I guess I should have said something. I'm not—you are not being dumped. That's not what I'm thinking at all."

"I don't know." I frowned at him, though maybe it wasn't as stern now that I was sighing like a contented kitty. "Two days of no word felt like it to me."

"Then you're wrong. I'm very very very interested. I can't even tell you how interested I am. I haven't been this hopeful about anything in…well you know how long."

"You have an awfully quiet way of expressing it."

His arms went around me, pulling me into an embrace. "I was thinking. God, I take too long to think now. I don't want to be a dick."

"I don't know what you're talking about."

"Bear with me a sec. It's hard to explain, but I'll try. I want you. I hope you know this."

The words and the actions matched so far. "Yes…"

"But I also know with shit stark clarity how what happened to you felt. I mean, it's not the same as mine—I actually think what happened to you was worse, but still, I know how it feels to be violated like that. Not that it's the same, because it's not exactly the same, but…are you with me?"

"Yes," and I was.

"So we met, and then we had our date, right, and I want you. I know that. I want you like I know how I want someone, but because of what happened to me—and you—I don't know what the next step is anymore. It's like I know what it should be, because I remember what it's like to be a guy who just wants to date a girl. But you're different, and I am too, and I don't trust my instincts anymore. I just know that I don't ever want to hurt you the way you've already been hurt. Is that crazy?"

I couldn't help it; I searched his face for signs of this being the most complicated "it's not you, it's me" speech ever. But I knew what he meant—that Incident sliced my life in half, into a Before and After. I was the same person who couldn't make decisions the same way.

Gio was trying to grasp the same for himself, but he didn't have Janine helping him come to terms with it, or even simply to find the words.

So he was trying to do that with many words.

"...if the surface tension's changed."

Words I didn't really understand. "What?"

"Like that experiment in high school, when you put things in water they actually float on the surface, but when you add something like detergent it changes the surface tension and some things start to sink..."

"We obviously didn't go to the same high school," I said, biting my lip. I'd only ever really interacted with babbling female scientists before. This was a little disorienting. "But I think I can catch up."

"I'll get there. Almost there. I'm the idiot who screwed up, a year ago. I don't have anyone to blame but myself. I did everything I could to distance myself from that but I don't know, because sometimes I still feel like that guy. So I'm here at this moment and I don't want to be that same guy with you. Especially you. And for two days I've been kicking myself because I think of what to do and what to say to you and it always seems like the wrong thing. Shit, this sounds—"

"I understand," I said. Maybe he wasn't doing the complicated dumping speech after all. But maybe it took being me to know it. "Did you ever get counseling after your incident?"

He shook his head. "But I need to, don't I?"

"That's your call," I told him. "I mean, you're trying to cope using science, I guess. Am I...detergent?"

"No, no—that's not what you are."

"I think I'll take that as a compliment? But we can establish some ground rules, I think. Moving forward. Tell each other how we want to be treated?"

"You'll need to help me out with that," Gio said.

"Let's just start with what's fair," I offered. "What I get, you get. What you ask me, I ask you. And take it from there?"

EIGHT

He asked the first difficult question. It wasn't deliberate, but the rhythm led to Gio getting the floor, and I let him have it. The walk back to my apartment was comfortable, easy, and we were almost silent except for the minor things we managed to say in between juggling *all the questions* in our heads.

"Are you hungry?" I'd said.
"Maybe I'll have a drink," he'd answered.
"I have beer. But it's just one bottle."
"We'll share it."
"Okay."

I only had two glasses in my kitchen, so I seemed halfway hospitable. We spent some seconds watching quietly as I poured the bottle's contents into them, and then I led him back to the couch, the original scene of our most recent crime.

"I don't usually get this beer."

He meant the dark lager we were having, the only kind I drank really. "It's my favorite."

"Good choice."

"Thanks."

Cute. Short. Nonsense. What do you talk about after you find out the most awful thing someone has been through?

When he sat on the couch he leaned all the way back, finding some way to rest his head. This flattened his hair against it, and I thought, *That's cute*. Which I thought was a good sign, that I could still think he was cute, even after.

Or a bad sign, a bad sign, because you should have learned.

I told my brain not to be so judgey. Again.

He turned his head toward me, and that was how it started. The drinks were gone before I knew it, and our hands were free, to hold another hand, free to press fingertips against arms, fabric, skin. I could have turned to kiss him and I didn't. He could have turned me toward him but he didn't. He did stretch out lengthwise on the couch and put his feet up, and pulled me in. The back of my shoulder was on his chest, each breath he took felt like a little nudge.

Tuesday was for talking.

"How did you find out?" Gio asked.

I had an answer for that question. I'd practiced how I might end up saying it to someone I loved. I was ready for it to be defensive, because in my head it was always in response to an accusation. But not now, not here. It was a question right in my ear, in the arms of the one asking, a voice over the beat of his heart. I could feel it. He was nervous.

And then I wasn't.

I was quiet a little longer than usual and he probably thought I wasn't ready. "Well, it can't be that bad," he said. "Or it can't be worse than mine."

"Oh, really? You want to do that? Because I think this is a game I can win."

"You're forgetting that I have nothing else to do all week. I hang out on the open field and randomly join football games."

"What are you talking about?"

"I'm competitive. Game on."

"Bradley, my ex-boyfriend, used his personal laptop at work," I told him. "His work laptop crashed and he brought in his personal one to give a presentation. One of the guys at the office who helped set it up copied from more folders than he should have."

"Shit."

"But your question was, how did I find out. I found out from Bradley, who found out from a friend at work. By the time we saw it, it had been on the website for a month."

His hand found mine, right over my hip, and our fingers twined. "Did the fucker go to jail?"

I shrugged. "He was fired. Bradley explored the kind of case he could file against him, but it was just some guy, and the damage was done. Eventually Bradley quit that job anyway. He just didn't want to deal with them anymore. We tried to go after the sites to have it taken down, but you probably know how that went."

I could feel him shaking his head. "It doesn't go away."

"Like pests." I took my own deep breath at this. "A bunch of people at his workplace saw it. Saw us. And they knew for a while, before anyone told him about it. I remember going to an office Christmas party of his, and now I get angry when I remember any faces from there. Even though I know it's not fair and most of them had nothing to do with it. Ugh."

He whistled, the sound and air of it moving past my hair. "That's shit."

God, this was all so comforting, so comfortable, even if the words were the ones that gave me hives. I missed being held. "Worse than your shit? How did *you* find out?"

"Well." Gio's leg bent and then stretched underneath mine.

"Are you *warming up*?"

"Ha. I guess I am. I don't think I've ever told this story in one go. *You* might need warming up."

"Right. Whatever."

"Vana—that's Leslie's sister—she called me, a few days after it happened. She follows the gossip blog that first posted the blind item about me and she knew it was me."

Vana, "Birthday Girl's Sister." I didn't twist around to look him in the eye. I was trying not to judge and if he saw me he was going to see *something* in my eyes, something I didn't want him to misinterpret. "Because it was her."

"Unfortunately." He pulled his hand away slightly.

I caught his fingers in mine and pulled them back in place. "On your girlfriend's birthday, you slept with her sister, and her friend."

"I did. But technically she was Vana's friend. Les doesn't like her."

I sighed. "So here's my question. How did *that* happen?"

"Oh god. I still ask myself that. There's no good answer."

"Do you know why?"

"I know *how*. You really want to hear this?"

"I wouldn't have asked if I didn't."

A pause, and I felt a kiss against the top of my head.

"This is going to make me sound like the biggest jerkface in this country."

"I think you already have that reputation, so you're not going to lose anything."

"You read about this? All of it?"

"Maybe most of it."

"It's not all true. Or whatever is true, they won't like it anyway."

"Were you actually having sex with your virgin girlfriend?"

He laughed a little, a bitter kind of laugh. "Not all the way but close enough. She and I wanted to, but she backed herself into a corner with the way her manager was pitching her—because she looks so angelic—and it messed with her head. 'Cause she's a good person, and she didn't want to be a liar."

"Too many people in the bedroom," I muttered.

"What?"

"Oh. That was something...that was how Bradley and I talked about this. When our relationship was getting toxic. *Too many people in the bedroom.* This was meant to be a private thing between the two of us, but suddenly there were too many opinions."

"Like that. Her manager, her parents, those people on the internet. We broke up a lot, in between. It was easier for her that way, especially because she was watched constantly. If I kissed her on the cheek she'd get comments about not staying pure and she'd need to give an interview or go to an orphanage or something."

"But you were at her birthday party."

"Well, that turned out to be genius," he said. "But yeah. That was a breakup that stuck. Almost a year, but I agreed to go to all of her public events so I'd look like a supportive boyfriend. I had to smile and shit but I couldn't talk to her or get too close. Isn't that fucked up?"

"She could have just announced that she was single."

"Yeah but she wasn't ready for it. I think we were both hoping it wasn't really over yet, but when it was, well, I couldn't stop showing up either."

"Did they pay you?"

"Of course not." He sighed. "I loved her. I didn't want to ruin things for her. And it was…it was a mall thing or a press conference here and there. Didn't take much of my time."

"You haven't explained how that all leads to a birthday threesome."

"It shouldn't have. Right? Nothing that came before it excuses it. All I can say is that I was horny and I hadn't gone on a real date with anyone for a long time, and I had to be at her birthday because she'd get bad press if I wasn't there. And Vana is great, a better friend even, since the thing with Les started falling apart, and we had always been flirting, and her friend was there…"

If I was wondering about it before, I wasn't anymore because I had my answer. The right time to talk about the worst sex shit you've ever done was right now, right before things got serious, right before you continue your courtship dance and present yourself as everything this person wanted you to be. Because a rejection this early would sting but you'd recover. The same information presented later would be betrayal and evisceration.

"Was it *good*?" I asked, smiling even if he couldn't see me.

"The threesome with my ex-girlfriend's older sister and her friend?"

"Yeah."

Throughout this I felt his arousal against my thigh; he'd gotten even harder. "I should mention again that I was horny as hell and had never really had sex, when it happened. I was so wired, it wasn't going to take a lot of convincing for me to do anything. And yeah, it was awesome. It was the best and worst night of my life."

"It sounds like it would be fun."

"Haha."

"Were you drunk? How safe were you?"

"Not at all drunk, and we used protection. They'd done this before, they knew what to do, had extra stuff with them. They liked…sharing. That's why they had photos. But someone screwed up and the photos got out."

I let that information sink in, closed my eyes even. I wasn't hurt by this. Not that it changed anything or made it okay, but he hadn't done it to me.

"I'm sorry," he said. "I didn't want to be that guy."

"You don't need to apologize to me," I told him, sincere about it, swear to God.

"I'm apologizing anyway."

"I think…I think you win."

"What?"

"You had it worse. I mean, I'm sure you enjoyed your threesome, but that was your first time. And it was documented and broadcast and you got called names for it. That's…I wouldn't know what I'd have done."

That would have freaked me out. But sometimes the grass was freakier on the other side of the fence.

"Huh," or maybe it wasn't so much a word, but the sound of Gio's throat clearing. "I might not like winning this game."

"It's not the best game."

"Too bad we're qualified to play it, huh?"

"Then why don't you go ahead and ask me the same question, and you can hear my answer."

"What was the question again?"

"How did it happen?" I said. *"How come you even had a sex video that could be leaked?"*

"Did you know you had a video, Iris?"

I nodded. "Yes. Because we took it."

"Do you like watching yourself?"

I pressed a hand against my forehead, because memories started coming and I don't know, maybe I thought I could push them back inside. But it was good to say it on my terms. "Do you know what hurt me the most when this was happening? I was told to blame this on Bradley. They wanted me to cry in public and say that I didn't know that I was being filmed, and that he betrayed me. I said, but it's not true, and how does that explain why he and I hadn't broken up, but it didn't matter to them. Just do it, they said. Bradley would be fine; he'd survive it. He wouldn't lose his job, wouldn't be called names, he'd be just another guy with a kink. But if I admitted that I was in on it, I'd lose everything."

"Did you lose everything?"

"My life is so different now. I'm not sure if I'm better off, sometimes. On good days I think I am."

"The dude is out of the picture anyway?"

"He left as soon as he could."

"Do you regret how you handled it? I mean, since you two broke up anyway. Like, did you think maybe you should have blamed him after all?"

Janine and I talked about this. On our first meeting even, and it was what convinced me to stay with her. "I think I would have felt worse if I lied," I said. "If I covered it up and pretended to be a victim, and made Bradley the guy who victimized me. That would have been worse, because it wasn't like that at all. And it would make me the person who stayed with the guy who betrayed her."

"But the truth hurt you."

It didn't destroy me. "I can't argue with it. Do you regret how you handled yours?"

"I wish they didn't take photos," Gio admitted. "But I can't say I wish it didn't happen. Even when Les was crying on TV, talking about how *I* had betrayed her. It made me feel like a dick but part of me was—*finally, I can move on*. I don't have to show up and be her good guy boyfriend anymore. She didn't like Vana very much either, so there was that too."

"Did you watch the video, Gio?"

"Yours? No."

Hmm. I wasn't sure how to deal with that information. Did I have to encourage him to watch it? Or did fairness require him not to, because I wouldn't have video of his to see...?

"Well, not yet at least," he added. "I don't have internet at my place so I had to go out to the net cafe to Google you. They had a filter, couldn't watch it. I don't know if I can, Iris."

"I'll understand if you do."

"It feels messed up."

"All of this is messed up." I checked the time; it was really late. "I have work tomorrow. I'm going to see you out now."

"Do I get to see you again?"

"Yes." Finally I turned around and kissed him, but it

was soft, and a proper good-night kiss if there ever was one. Which he responded to in an equally sweet, proper way.

He looked grateful. And *ready*. "So I was thinking of taking you out to dinner."

"A date?"

"I think we deserve it."

I agreed with him.

NINE

"Do you like watching yourself?"

When I moved quite suddenly from marketing to spreadsheet/database/generally-unseen person, I found strange comfort in the database of scholarship applications.

At first, Miley and Carl went through every form. This entire foundation was a sibling pet project, and they started by convincing their family to put up the beginnings of the fund. Later, when that wasn't enough, they figured out how to involve corporations, other science orgs, other rich families, to help keep the fund going and send young women interested in science and math to college and beyond. The team grew because there *were* a lot of applicants, many who would go the distance on this if given a chance. When I interned for them in college, as a management and development major who hadn't really figured out what she wanted to do, I saw those applications come in but only printed them out and filed them.

After The Incident, it became my job to read them. There were internal guidelines to make the longlist for any given grant per year, and sometimes the guidelines were different depending on who was giving the money and the kind of student they wanted to support. I went through transcripts, documentation of family finances, and essays. Oh those essays.

It was hard to tell what I'd end up reading on any given work day, but I looked forward to those essays. We didn't judge them on literary merit, but we did ask them to say something about themselves, what they intended to do, and why use this particular path to do it. On some days, I'd get a confused, awkward mess, and I'd need to work harder to find the message behind it. On other days, I'd be moved to tears and I'd wish the powers that be give her all the money she asked for.

Sometimes the essay questions were different, depending on the grant.

Sometimes as I printed them out and prepared them for review of my bosses and the donors, I imagined writing these essays about myself.

Explaining myself.

Why didn't you let your then-boyfriend take the fall for you, Iris Len-Larioca? Please state your answer in 500 words or less.

When I was growing up, I was taught to always tell the truth. Still, I wasn't the easiest person to raise. I was the child who was always getting yelled at: I didn't put things back, never wanted to go where they wanted me to, wasn't ready on time. I was difficult, but I never lied.

I didn't blame Bradley for all of this, because it felt wrong. The sex was consensual. The decision to record it was, too. I understood that the truth could be painful but it was also *better*. I saw it in my brother's life, and I was ready to believe that if I ever needed to choose. And yet those who raised me to do this were the first to tell me to give it up, to save their own faces.

Why are you still in town then, making it difficult for them who are ashamed of you now, Iris Len-Larioca? Please state your answer in 500 words or less.

Exile was the path Bradley took, and I knew that most of my family wanted me to do the same. I wish it had been for me, because I would be safer, happier, elsewhere, but I knew that my welfare was the last thing on their minds.

Why did you take a video of yourself having sex, Iris Len-Larioca? Please state your answer in 500 words or less.

This, I didn't need even a dozen words on.

I didn't know.

That was a hell of a lot of consequences to bear for something I didn't know or was unwilling to understand.

We regret to inform you that you did not receive this grant at this time, I told myself, giving my answer the standard rejection. *But don't give up! You can always try again.*

That last part was never in the letters, but I thought that for them, every time.

"I DON'T KNOW. What would you have done as a second date?"

Gio and I were already at a milestone in our strange little experiment—we were together, outdoors, and right at the entrance of the mall in the NV Park complex. I worked a slightly earlier shift that Friday so we could meet at a decent dinner hour, and there we were, at eight in the evening, looking at "Enter Here" like it was a monster's mouth that was going to swallow us up.

I wish I had worn something nicer. I was in the same black and white striped dress I'd gone to work in, and only stopped by my apartment to switch bags, brush my hair, and add a layer of cologne to myself. He looked great in jeans and a dark blue shirt, the collar a subtle V, revealing just enough down his throat that I knew what I was going for the first chance I got.

"A movie," Gio said. "I'd ask you out to a movie."

That sounded like something normal people would do.

"Let's do that," I said.

There were two movies we were right in time for: a Filipino romantic comedy, and an American horror movie that had a horrible poster. He pointed to the romcom, and I pointed to the horror movie.

"Cute," I told him. "Now let's try this again and be honest."

Our fingers switched posters.

Gio was laughing. When he laughed, most of his distracting eyes hid behind lids and lashes. "How do we settle this?"

"It doesn't matter which one, really."

"Well, if you don't care anyway. There's a guy in the Pinoy movie that I don't like."

"Former friend of yours?"

"Not at all. Always hated his guts."

His hand closed around mine. It was warmer than when we last touched digits, or maybe because I was smiling this time, and he could see me. I wondered what I looked like, when I was smiling. I didn't have anything like those eyes of his to distract people with.

Holding hands would have been nothing, but for those few minutes and throughout the movie, they were everything to me again. You couldn't have quizzed us on what the movie was about. Instead it was an hour of various stages of handsiness. His right hand and my left together on the arm rest between us. Later, pinkies hooked, backs of hands resting against each other. Then his right hand on my back, slowly going up, then down, on a path parallel to the zipper on my dress.

This movie idea was a joke, but I was in on it. I leaned back into his hand, and turned my head to find his mouth. Good thing he didn't care about the movie either because he kissed like he didn't want to know where the vengeful ghost was going to pop up next. The theater wasn't even full, not that many people cared either.

But I bet the others inside weren't kissing like we were.

I bet they weren't kissing like they literally hadn't kissed anyone else in at least a year. Like they were making up for other second dates, other movie makeout sessions missed, other random Friday nights they could have been kissing someone else but weren't. God knows I was zipping right through all the kisses I deserved in November, December, January, February...

I'd never made out in a movie theater before. It wasn't as dark as I thought it would be, didn't offer the kind of cover and privacy I thought it would. But that wasn't the point, was it, you didn't pay money to sit in a seat and grope someone in surround sound. You kissed your date in there because you couldn't wait to get out, couldn't take sitting that close, the smell of him mixed with a faint popcorn scent, couldn't take that your hands had nowhere else to go but on each other.

Gio paused to breathe. "You like kissing."

Ha, I didn't even *need* the break. "You're not bad at it."

"Thanks."

"Why did we stop?"

"Do you want to get out of here?"
"Oh my god, yes."

LET'S get out of here—easy to say, easy to do, but it wasn't cut to my apartment, taking his clothes off. In reality, it was five minutes of individually retreating to the cinema bathroom to make ourselves presentable, fix rumpled clothing, comb through mussed hair. Then meeting again in front of the bathrooms, looking about as sheepish as teenagers who'd been caught making out at a movie.

It was so cute though. Sheepish was a feeling I still got but never tried to show to other people anymore. Trying to be strong and unaffected about everything took away little emotions like this.

Gio had an "oh shit" smile on his face and it was adorable. "I can't believe we did that."

"Can't believe we did what?"

"I'd finish the movie I was making out to, at least."

I giggled. "Life's too short."

"I agree with you there," he said. "Do you want to go back home?"

Home. Right.

"Let's take the long way back," I told him. "I want to ask you a few things...before we end up home."

The long way wasn't to go back the way we'd come in and cross the street to the residential towers. It was a route that I'd created, and I didn't expect him to know it, but he followed me out anyway.

"This is how I go to the field," he said. "Especially when it's raining."

There was a way to go around all of NV Park without

stepping out into the sun or rain, but it was circuitous and complicated. But at least you could go anywhere, and get home despite the elements. It was also, tellingly, a path that avoided many open spaces. Chances to be recognized.

"Are we crazy?" Oh. I placed a hand over my mouth after I said that, because in my mind it was *Am I crazy?* and it wasn't supposed to include him at all.

"Are you chickening out?" he answered, a little too quickly. "Because I'm not."

"*Why?*"

"Why am I not chickening out? Why are you asking this?"

"Because it seems like I'd be the wrong person for you right now."

"Are you kidding me?"

I wasn't.

He realized I wasn't. "You're wrong if you think I'm going to be scared off by that. By what happened to you."

"Is this the first date you've been on since your...incident?"

"I guess it is, yeah."

"Is this the first time you've been physical with someone since your threesome?"

"Yes, but—"

"We can't rebound with each other. It's not right. It's not right to find the person who has the worse breakup story and then rebound with them."

"Hey. Hey." Gio was suddenly catching up to me because I'd inadvertently begun walking faster, like away from him. "Stop. Back up. We'll talk about this. Can I object? No, I will anyway. Okay. This is the first time you've kissed someone since your thing?"

"Yeah," I admitted.

"But yours was two years ago."

"Yours was more recent."

"Yes, and *that* was my rebound, Iris. I got out of that thinking, shit, this is insane, and I don't need this or any of these people for a good long while. My family—I love them, but damn they're the stuff of TV dramas and I wanted to be the different one. Of course the only time I really fuck up and it gets on the news."

"I'm sorry that—"

"That part of my life is over. I quit my job because I worked with them. I moved here because I lived with them. Les I haven't seen in a long time, but Vana tried to keep in touch and I said we shouldn't. I didn't date. I didn't sleep around. It's a year later and I'm alive. It took a while to make sure I was fine with it, but I needed to make sure that I could live without that shitstorm. Do you think a year isn't long enough to realize things?"

Oh god. So many things, so many questions leading to more questions. How could he just do that? Why did it take me so long? What was his secret?

"I want you," he said. "And I don't want to hurt you. I am in for whatever you're ready for. What is it you're really asking me? You can be honest with me."

I wanted to be. I told myself I would be, but it was hard. "It's that…"

"Be honest. You can do it. You already know the worst thing I've ever done."

"I want to sleep with you tonight," I blurted out. "And I don't want you to wake up thinking it was your worst anything."

Oh my god. Oh my god. I said it. My fingers covered my

lips, covered the sheepish smile that was forming there. He took that cover away and pressed a kiss on my smile.

"Is that it?" Gio said. "I can assure you that's not going to be a problem at all."

TEN

"How do you take this off?"

"Here."

"Let me."

His place. His bedroom. His hands looking for the zipper that would release me from my dress.

His mattress. A little softer than what I was used to, but this wasn't about my spine health. This was me in my black bra and panties, lying on another guy's bed, for the first time since you-know-what. Counting breaths.

"Don't worry about that," he'd said, when I made a move to take his shirt off for him. When I went for his belt buckle instead. When I'd attempted to undress myself. Instead I was made to lie back and wait, and my hands grabbed at his bedsheets in anticipation. He undressed like he was in no hurry, so annoying. First releasing his belt, hanging it up on a hook behind his bedroom door. Then pulling his shirt off, throwing it toward a corner of the room and right into a laundry basket. Pants off, and then draped over a chair next to the bed.

I bit into my thumb to suppress a giggle and didn't quite

succeed.

"What?" Gio asked, blessedly making it to the foot of his own bed, only in boxers.

"You're neat."

"Usually."

I could look at him all night, all parts of him. He seemed to be totally okay with being shirtless, and there was so much for me to see, but those eyes drew me in again. Didn't think I'd be into eyes, of all things, so instead I let my hands explore everything else. He crawled over me and I touched his shoulders first, then pressed my palms against his chest.

I loved this part. I mean, I enjoyed what we were about to do in general, but this part—that first time, when you're both discovering each other—was exhilarating, and it wouldn't happen again.

That moment when you're introducing yourself to someone in this way. When you do so reverently, when you're sober, when you're not in a rush.

It's the best.

He was kissing my throat, taking his time there, his tongue making lazy sweeps down my collar bone, toward my chest. I took that time to check out his waist, the feel of his hips, solid where I knew mine would be softer. With a snap the straps that secured my bra went limp, and my breath caught when his mouth captured a nipple and his hands cradled my breasts.

Still good. This wasn't ruined yet, for me.

"You're gorgeous," he was saying between licks. "Unbelievably gorgeous."

I could believe him. Or if I didn't, maybe I already did by the time he had moved on to my other breast, which he may have liked even more because it got way more attention. But I needed his mouth on mine, I needed to kiss him so I yanked him up and higher by the hair and claimed the lips that had been wandering for too long. Like this, I was able to press up against him, felt the friction, the heat of his skin behind those last layers of fabric that separated us.

He loved my hair, loved seeing it on his sheets, loved the tips brushing against his arms when he had flipped us over and had me on top. This was how he entered me, protected by latex, hips pushing up. My hair on his skin tickled, he said later, like a breeze, different from the heady pleasure of enduring my tongue, my teeth, my nails.

Because I was on him, and I gave as good as I got. It was lust, it was energy, it was...relief. He was hard and slick and full. I loved his slow thrusts like I loved lazy Sundays, because they felt luxurious and warm and like they could last forever. I craved his quick thrusts because they were *perfect*, they were extraordinarily efficient, like I knew I'd get there and in how many strokes if he kept it up.

He loved my tongue too, loved that thing I did when he had pushed himself up so we were upright, on the bed, connected still, and I was Frenching him to match how he pulsed inside me. This was much later, and here, when I realized that this was how I wanted to let go. Kissing him, wrapped around him, and I warned him I would.

"Like this?" he gasped. "God, yes, now."

And I did, moaning into his mouth, grinding into him, into his quick thrusts. I was hanging on to him like this, still lazily kissing him, when I felt him pull out and come.

It was sweat, and lips, and it was still all good.

Thank goodness.

"SO," I told him, as I tapped my disposable fork over the lid of my cup noodles. "I usually come here and buy food when I'm hungry at two a.m. and there are other people here when I do that. It's never really empty."

Gio was mixing powdered creamer into his brewed coffee. "Night shift. Makes sense. And the convenience stores are still open at this hour."

"Didn't really think about how many of them were going out for a snack after sex."

This guy, this adorable blue-eyed guy I'd just had sex with, and was now having snacks with, started laughing. His coffee sloshed in his cup and a drop spilled onto the tabletop. "Why stop at two a.m.? People are probably having sex at noon, when they take off for lunch."

I smiled. "Afternoon coffee breaks."

"Quickies before dinner. You can get a room by the hour, so it's convenient for everyone." After a sip from a more stable cup, he added, "I used to think about that. How everyone was getting to have all this fun sex whenever they wanted, everyone but me."

"But I thought you were getting some action with your ex. Weren't you?"

He paused, probably deliberating how much to share. Not that I needed him to. I already had what I considered too much information about his ex-girlfriend, and while that was a curiosity and novelty last week, today I felt like scrubbing my brain, if I could. It didn't help that I could imagine, for example, that "no sex" probably did not exclude oral, and that they were probably doing everything short of the actual, to get each other off.

"It's different," he said, choosing to be vague. "Yeah, we were fooling around, but it was hard to enjoy it. She was never really alone with me. And if we were, when we were done, it's like...everyone knew what we were up to."

We were sitting on stools, on the same side of a white plastic table, facing the windows of the 24/7 store. Maybe we still looked exactly how we did when we lined up to get movie tickets—same outfits, down to the shoes. The hair though, the way his was sort of randomly sticking up in bunches in the back, the way mine was heavy with the residue of dried sweat. I reached out to smooth his hair down, but it bounced right back up once my fingers let go.

"The people who know what you were doing are the ones who already have that in the brain," I said. "You could have been playing chess in a locked room and they would have been thinking it."

"That's nice, if we were actually playing chess."

This was making me remember my own short history with sex. It had only ever been with Bradley, though he wasn't my first boyfriend. He was the guy right before we graduated from college, and we only were as adventurous as we had been because it looked like it was going to be only him, always.

Not true.

"How old are you now, Gio?"

"Twenty-three. Why, how old are you?"

"Twenty-four." Despite it being stubborn, I tried smoothing his hair down again.

"Do you feel old?" Gio asked me. "Because of what happened?"

"I don't know. Maybe? Because I wasn't having a lot of fun for a long time."

"I moved here because I knew someone who was letting go of the apartment, of 9J," Gio said. "He was a few batches ahead of me in college. Now that I took his place, I've been hanging out with his friends and they're a little older than me, and I like it."

"How much older?"

"Four, five years. They're cool. But it might be because they're not related to anyone I know, or they're just handling life better. I was sitting in toxic shit for so long, I didn't even know it."

"You mean the girlfriend in show business?"

"The girlfriend in show business. The manager. Her sister who's cool, but actually kind of liked me. Their brother who will probably beat me up senseless when he next sees me. Their parents, who are Country Club brunch buddies with my parents by the way, and also business partners, so this screw-up of mine made everything complicated. And then there's that network executive who really, really wanted her to be the virgin role model, and that other dude in her show who kept hitting on her, and that gossip blog that kept posting photos of us together..."

"Wow," I said. "That birthday threesome was a disaster waiting to happen."

"I didn't want it to be me. I mean it's messed up, but I didn't want to be the cause of it."

It was late and we were tired, so he could have just been tired. Or that was actual anguish there, weighing on those shoulders, hovering, bearing down on him.

"At least you're free. Are you happier?"

"Yes." He faced me and rested his face into the curve of my neck. It was unexpected and it tickled, but I faced the glass and watched us there instead.

"Wow, that fast, huh?"

"Not fast at all. You're okay?"

"Yes. Yes, I am."

"I think this is a good second date then."

I nudged him a little, and our combined silhouette moved together, then back again. "I agree."

ELEVEN

After convenience store snacking, we walked back to Tower 3, to our floor, and he walked me to my door and gave me a really nice, coffee-flavored kiss. Then it was good night, and an offer to take me out to lunch.

"I have lunch plans," I said. "With neighbors."

"Coffee then," he offered. "Before your lunch. And outside. When it's sunny."

"I don't burst into flames in sunlight."

"If I drop by your place with coffee I know what I'll want to do instead," he told me, nuzzling the words into my ear. "And sometimes I really do just want coffee."

"Knock," I said. "I'll go with you if I'm awake."

"Awesome."

"You should get a phone or something."

Gio shrugged, not sorry. "I'm not there yet. I sure am glad you're just down the hall."

"Good night, Gio."

"Good night, Iris."

It felt a little like college.

I'd been sharing an apartment with two friends near the

university, and Bradley was in a dorm on campus. That was an entire flirtation and relationship that had been based on proximity, knowing that person could be there early in the morning or late at night. The idea of moving back to our own homes, taking jobs that meant we wouldn't see each other every day, I remember being a little afraid of it. I knew that other friends broke up with their college boyfriends after a few years, if they hadn't settled down yet.

We'd probably clung to each other too tightly to prevent from growing apart.

Would we have broken up, eventually, if The Incident hadn't happened? It was hard to look back now and decide, depending on how much I wanted to punish myself, how wrong or right our relationship had been. It wasn't perfect— he went out with his new work friends too much, I threw myself into my job and got less and less annoyed when the daily dinners became three times a week, then weekly. But we'd get hit by guilt that we were neglecting each other, and rebound with a weekend at a hotel or something.

The videos that got out were from one of those weekends. We argued about something stupid that week, and as per usual made up by overcompensating on everything. Not just makeup sex, but a weekend of it, a lot of it, and on video.

It felt like so long ago. It wasn't.

But this, before I ruined it by overthinking myself into misery, was the *good part* of feeling like college. It was new, and cute. And fun. Gio and I deserved new, and cute, and fun, after what we'd been through. Right? How long could we keep this up?

I was already dressed when I heard his knock.

"Good morning, Gio."

"Good morning, Iris."

Our kisses tasted minty, perfectly acceptable for the morning after the first time. Showed we still cared.

"What's your favorite coffee place?" he asked.

"Take me to yours."

Because the NV Park complex had a lot of coffee places. You'd think it would be all the same, but no; you could throw your environmentally-responsible paper cup of coffee across the street and hit another branch of a different establishment, serving nearly the exact same thing. But Gio had a favorite place, and he bought two of his favorite pour-over blend, and we walked back to Tower 3 with warm cups in our hands.

"Your Saturdays are like this?" I asked him.

"Yeah. My first meal's lunch, but I get coffee in the morning. And I walk. I like walking."

I liked walking with him. Sun against his face. I got to let him walk a little bit ahead of me and I checked out his butt in those jeans. Nice.

Normal.

We entered the Tower 3 lobby and the guards pointed to the right. To the reception area, where there were seats, and a young woman who was standing and looking at us.

"Kimmy," Gio said, his back tensing up.

Who was she? I would have reacted like that if I'd seen an ex, but we were on the wrong side of so many people, it could have been anyone.

"Kimmy" was a gorgeous corporate queen bee, if there ever was one. Tailored dress in deep purple, tall shoes making her taller, hair blown out like there was a breeze on her, but still and perfect. She smiled at him, then me, and walked closer, offering her cheek.

"Good morning, Gio," she said.

"What do you want?" he asked.

She didn't find that rude at all, even if it sounded like it would be. "I need help again."

"Ask your boyfriend to help you."

"Oh come on," Kimmy said, pulling two small boxes out of her bag. "You know your big brother can't be bothered with the chemistry of this."

Gio looked at me, then her, then shifted his feet like he would rather be somewhere else. "What exactly is it again?"

"Awesome." Kimmy displayed the two little red boxes in each hand—lipstick, still in their packaging. "Bella Mariel's new lip line. They tell me they won't reformulate, this is final. I'll need you to explain certain things to me. Like why only colors that don't match any of my outfits, why it ends up on Manolo's mouth when I kiss him. You still helped them with this, right?"

He didn't make a move to pick up the boxes. "I didn't make it for them, but I helped them meet regulations on the claims for natural and organic. There's documentation in the office, you can just get it."

"I don't have time to read all the paperwork, Gio. I don't even have time right now for the conversation of you explaining why. I'll drop by Monday afternoon and you explain to me over coffee, okay?"

He narrowed his eyes. "Same rate?"

Then Kimmy's eyes narrowed too. "But you're just explaining something over coffee."

"It's a seminar. I'd be paid hourly to deliver a seminar."

"It's coffee and being helpful to your future sister-in-law, wiseass."

"Go get a chemical engineering degree and read the report yourself, then."

Kimmy bit her lip and started shaking her head, but it was a battle already lost. "Fine. Your hourly rate. Don't think I don't know that I'm keeping you in your hermit lifestyle."

"Deal. See you on Monday."

"Fabulous." Then she turned to me, her smile curious. "Hello. I'm Kimmy."

"Yeah, I heard. Iris," I said.

She took my hand and pressed the lipstick boxes into my open palm. "You take these. And you test them. Tell me I'm not wrong, these things look and feel and smell great, but they're all over a guy during a makeout session. That's not the tagline they're looking for, I'm sure."

Not exactly how I wanted to score some free makeup, but I could only nod, and stuff them into my pocket, while my face blushed a natural red.

"I have to go," I told them. Actually I could have only really been talking to Gio, but Kimmy was right there, so I guess she was part of it too. "I need to...go to my thing."

"All right." And he kissed me, on the mouth, in front of his brother's future wife. I was a little surprised, but then told myself, why wouldn't he? We weren't hiding. This was a totally normal thing.

TWELVE

Because Matilda and I were now friends who had each other's numbers, I found out the modern way that she wanted me to go to her apartment instead at 14F.

See, this was a lot more efficient than leaving pieces of paper under doors.

The higher up our building you went, the bigger the apartment cuts were. Less units crammed per floor. I didn't mind the limited space of the one-bedroom I had; it was just enough for me. It was also at the very, very edge of what I could afford. I splurged on extra square meters of space while someone might have decided to get new shoes instead.

Matilda, I noticed as soon as I walked into her place, splurged on square meters instead of a closetful of things. She had a two-bedroom, two-bathroom unit, and from in here you could walk out onto a real mini balcony, instead of the fake one on the other side of my living room window.

"Wow," I said. "You got a great one here."

She welcomed me in, wearing a glittery robe over her white tank top and white shorts, both underdressed and over the top at the same time. I had a feeling this was exactly the way she wanted it.

"This place? This isn't the goal yet, but it'll do." She kissed my cheek and ushered me past the kitchen, around the coffee table/living room, and toward the sunny dining area, where two other people were already sitting.

One of them was Kimmy, as in Gio's future sister-in-law.

"Ladies," Matilda said, raising a glittery sleeve theatrically. "This is Iris. Iris, Kimmy and Mosh."

"We met," Kimmy said, her smile even more curious and sly. "Downstairs. She was with Gio."

Matilda clapped her hands, unable to contain her glee. "I knew it. I knew it. I mean, she told me, but of course I didn't go like this right then so it won't freak her out. Iris, I'm happy to introduce you to my BISHes, Kimmy Domingo and Mosh Chavez. We meet every Saturday, if we can, and I hope we don't freak you out so much that you stop going."

I didn't hear that right the first time. Of course I thought she said "bitches."

Mosh looked about my age, petite next to Kimmy the giant Barbie, and her hair was in an updo but that couldn't conceal that it was shades of gold. "She probably thinks you said 'bitches,' Mats," she said, smiling as she pointed to the empty chair beside her. "Don't offend our new guest."

"I have a feeling she doesn't offend easily," Matilda said, grabbing a glass from the table and gulping down whatever was in it, in one motion. "Iris, we call ourselves BISHes. B. I. S. H. Beautiful. Independent. Survivors of Humiliation."

My mouth dropped open.

Kimmy raised her glass to me. "Welcome to the club."

LUNCH WAS GREAT. Matilda served salmon. And salad. And fancy cheeses. And red wine.

And I met the BISHes.

Sometime between fancy cheeses and dessert, I began to wonder what my therapist would think of this. I'd told her that I felt I couldn't talk to anyone, and didn't want to. It was so tricky, opening up to people about this, and it wasn't even their fault because most of them I knew for a long time and predicted exactly how they wouldn't understand. My friends would *never* allow themselves to be filmed in the act. My brother would be supportive, but wouldn't stop trying to get me back into the house. My parents were understandably disappointed and will never be talking about this for the rest of their lives. I vaguely remembered Janine mentioning if I needed a support group, but I dismissed it quickly. I mean, I didn't even know what I needed, wasn't sure which keywords to search.

Then this, and it clicked in my head.

Because other people were telling me how to feel, and I never felt totally right about it. I was betrayed by a loved one, they said. I was victimized by an amateur porn site, they said. I was violated by the journalists who sensationalized the few news items about this, they said. It could have been true, but those words didn't nail the feeling.

This word did: *humiliation.*

Truth—something about that word unburdened me. Something that had been heavy and tightly wound inside of me began to unravel throughout lunch, as I sat there and listened to Matilda, Kimmy, and Mosh. I spoke little, absorbed more.

Humiliation.

That was it. That was it.

They had been friends for years and knew each other's back stories. They didn't mind recapping for the newbie though. They talked while passing each other salad and refilling glasses of wine, talked about their *humiliation* like they were talking about an adorable puppy video. Did you see this? Have you heard about the thing?

I'd never gotten around to Googling Matilda Ruiz, but she told me what was up with her anyway.

"I was with a nasty, ugly, hateful man for three years," she said. "So I could live in a penthouse unit in this very building and not have to work."

"You made candles," Mosh reminded her. "You sold them at bazaars and shit."

"That didn't pay my rent," Matilda said with a shrug. "My boyfriend paid my rent."

That he did, until she got back to that penthouse unit one day and was told that she needed to move out. Matilda knew what that meant, knew she was being broken up with, and out of spite hurled her lit candles at him and started a small fire. Curtains got singed, the fire department came, but she did manage to "move out" of his life that day.

"You should have left when you first needed to go to an ER," Kimmy said. "You should have told me when you first went to an ER."

"Penthouse," Matilda retorted. "And I didn't have a plan yet then."

I watched how they talked to each other, waited for that tone of "you should have known better." But it wasn't that; it was, *yeah, I should have known better. Fuck that.*

After that story, I was relieved to know that Kimmy was actually quite happy and functional in her relationship—since this guy was, after all, Gio's brother. She had her own

PR firm and the Mella family's cosmetics company was a new client.

"Trust me, I didn't want to be working for them in any way," Kimmy said. "But whatever. Eventually I'll be part of that business, might as well help them with it."

"Are you calling yourself engaged now?" Mosh asked.

Matilda laughed. "No. She's not even wearing the ring."

Kimmy rolled her eyes at them and flashed a ringless hand at me. "Before Manolo and I got together, I was supposed to marry someone else. He called it off days before the wedding."

"Oh my god," I said.

She nodded. "Hey, I'm fine. What stings about that whole thing isn't that I regret losing him—everyone involved in that mess is happily with someone else—but people thought I deserved it, you know?"

"Why would they think that?" I asked.

"Because she's a beautiful woman who speaks her mind and takes no prisoners," Matilda said.

Kimmy winked. "Because I'm a bitch."

See, I was called that, on the internet, even before anyone who watched porn knew my name. Kimmy Domingo did not sound like she felt sorry for herself or anyone though.

"I don't like weak people," she said, like she was revising her self-description. "I don't have the patience for them. It means a lot of people were waiting for something like that to happen to me, and they got to have their fun."

"That's over," she said. "Mosh's drama isn't over."

I didn't know what that meant. Until it was explained to me that Mosh was Monica Laura Topaz Chavez...

"...oh," I said. Even I knew of her father, accomplice then whistleblower to a government funds scandal, who only recently died of a heart attack, while still under investigation.

"Oh yes," Mosh said, now raising her glass to us. "That's me."

It was true, apparently, her family *was* acquiring wealth that it didn't deserve. She was investigated too, briefly, but she was cleared and agreed to cooperate. But that didn't help her situation all that much. She was an artist and children's rights advocate who now couldn't find work with the same groups that needed her for fundraising and awareness, because her name was too toxic. She was also very recently unemployed again.

My numerous and rejected resignation letters should be ashamed of themselves.

"What do you do now?" I asked her.

"I don't know yet," she said. "Right now I'm here with you and I'm drinking wine in the daytime."

"You don't have to tell us your story, Iris," Matilda said. "This isn't show and tell. It's not about that."

"So what's it about?" I asked.

Matilda sighed, and thought about it. Her robe fell down one shoulder, drooped down her chair. "Silence. A space where there's no judgment."

Kimmy shook her head. "Productive judgment."

Mosh's glass clinked against the table. "Wine."

IF KIMMY and Matilda were friends, then Kimmy knew my Incident. When Mosh excused herself to use the bathroom and Matilda checked her refrigerator for the status of the next bottle of wine, Kimmy hopped over to the chair beside me.

"You and Gio?" she said.

"It's really new," I told her.

"I've known them since we were kids," Kimmy said. "Manolo, Gio, the family. Gio, since he was born."

"Okay."

"He's a good guy."

"Seems like it."

"I think I should qualify that. I know the family, and I love them, but they can be...another level entirely. Naked diving into pools kind of level. One of their cousins was missing for two years and showed up at Christmas with a wife and five adopted kids. Another took off for a summer and ended up in a Bollywood movie as a villain, left her husband for her co-star. Wildly entertaining sometimes, and fucked up when it's bad. Gio is—he's probably the only one of them who was straight-up good guy for so long. He was never any trouble."

"Until his threesome got on the internet, right?"

Kimmy laughed. "I wouldn't have guessed that would be his intro to the next level, no."

"He's apparently very competitive."

"Oh god. They're hilarious. I mean, you need to have a sense of humor about these things. It...kind of makes sense though."

The threesome made sense? I raised an eyebrow but said nothing.

"It gives me the creeps to think of him as a sexual creature, but look. He was being the virgin boyfriend will-wait-for-marriage guy and maybe he didn't want to be. You can't keep that under for too long. It's going to get out."

"I think he feels bad enough about it as it is."

"He's only hard on himself because he can't believe he can rise—or stoop—to the level of his cousins. Or his brother. Although that stunt beats anything Manolo ever got caught for."

"His privacy was violated," I said. "It's not easy to get over that."

Her eyes sort of narrowed, focused, probably remembered the source of my words and the pain behind it. "Right," she said. "Of course. It's good for him to know though that he's not alone, that his people still care for him. His...*needs* aside, he hasn't lost anything. He has a place in that family if he wants to go back."

I wasn't sure what to say to this, but I kept thinking, good for him. Good for him.

"Anyway," Kimmy said. "If he were in this room today that's what I'd tell him. That he shouldn't feel shame. That shame is useless to himself and others. Don't you think so, Iris?"

"Shame is someone else's way of putting you into a box, to control you, and take away what you could have," Matilda declared, swooping back in with new wine. "But it's useful for something."

"And that is?" Kimmy demanded.

"It can give you a goal," Matilda said.

"You and your goals," Kimmy teased.

"I believe in that," Matilda told me. "Own the thing that someone used to humiliate you. Then you overcome it. You know what my goal is? A penthouse unit in this same building. But my own money."

"You're one floor away," I said.

"Almost there." Matilda nodded toward her friend. "Kimmy here should get over her fear of telling people she's about to get married."

"I'm not afraid of it."

"Right. You don't wear your engagement ring. You don't

call him your fiancé. Your man is hopeless for you and you know it, but you won't let it show."

"Matilda thinks we need to go full circle on things for closure," Kimmy said. "I say, do whatever you need to do to keep your head up. And small weddings are better anyway."

"Mosh needs to get a job again. Doing the exact thing she loves, with people who aren't afraid of associating with her," Matilda said. "And you, Iris, you need—"

"Don't tell her what she needs," Kimmy scolded. "She'll come up with that herself, *mom*."

What do you need, Iris? 500 words or less.

That piece of cheese looked really good, so I put that in my mouth, instead of saying anything.

THIRTEEN

When I went to work on Monday, I was wearing new lipstick. Kimmy had given me two, and this was the softer pink labeled 497. It was the kind of color that was barely there, because it closely matched my own lips, but I wore it with conviction. Look at this girl—friends, sex, new lipstick.

Life was happening again.

Gio recognized it as soon as I kissed him. I found a message for me at the Tower 3 lobby, asking me to head over to a chicken inasal place at the mall if I wanted to have dinner with him. So I did, and there we were. What Kimmy said was true though; I'd needed to reapply the lipstick several times throughout the day, and did another touch-up right before I headed over to dinner.

"You taste like work," he said, a tiny shred of it sounding like a complaint. "I was talking about this product all afternoon."

"You taste like chicken."

"Did you want some? I ate ahead, didn't know if you'd get my message in time."

I shook my head. "Had a late snack. You should call me and invite me to dinner."

He shook his head. "I call you and other people can call me. Phones are doors and windows to madness."

"Seriously," I scooted onto the bench next to him, inhaling grilled chicken-, garlic-, and vinegar-scented smoke. "You can ignore a phone if you want to."

"Not in my experience. Not when you know the people I know."

Well. Nonstop calling, texting, emailing, asking how he was. Didn't that just mean more concerned people, more loved ones? It didn't work that way for me. There was nothing newsworthy about my family. My dad and mom met in a logistics and shipping company, that my dad still worked for to this day. Other relatives were in banks, insurance companies, and food companies. They made things, answered phones, delivered things. They weren't talked about as much as other families, I guess.

"Fine," I said. "So, you were working. Kimmy, right? You were an employed chemical engineer today?

"Yeah. So you just learned how I can afford to keep living alone."

I'd learned a lot of things about you, I wanted to say. I mean the Google crawl alone was already too much information to process, but the conversation with Kimmy was also telling, because she was right there in his world and not an anonymous web commenter. I appreciated what she shared, because she seemed to be a good person, but all Sunday I kept wondering if I were better off not knowing most of this. Or of discovering all of it on my own. This chicken restaurant was a glorified cafeteria, but they served good stuff. Would I have thought Gio was a cheapskate if he invited me here? Would he have taken me somewhere else even if he couldn't afford to? How would we have found out all these other little things? Would it have mattered?

That was another thing that had been taken away from us—the right to start over.

"Did Kimmy tell you that she's my friend now?"

Gio did not know that. So she wasn't going around giving him recaps of everything. "How did that happen?"

"My new friend from the building, her name's Matilda. She's friends with Kimmy. Small world, huh?"

"She knows a lot of people. I did ask for her help looking for an apartment, when I took off. You're okay? Did she say anything weird?"

"Weird like what?"

"Weird like whatever you found on the blogs plus a family tree." Gio was done with his meal by now, and was wiping his greasy fingers on a scrap of tissue.

"She mentioned a few examples of…adventurous things your family's done."

The sound that came out of him was a lot like disapproval. "It's not as funny as she thinks it is. Not many people are ready for it."

"I don't need to meet them at all," I offered. "And if I do…well, you know I can't judge."

"Thank you. Doesn't change how I'm not proud of being part of that."

What do you need, Gio? I wondered. It was hard for me to believe that he really meant that. Surely this hermit stage was a stage, the way I knew my own hiding in this complex would eventually come to an end.

"Well now you know everything about me," he said, "and I know nothing about everything else about you. I don't like that."

"Oh. Of course. Because you're competitive?"

"Because if you know anything about my family then you can't take me seriously."

"Poor you." I kissed his nose. "How do I make you feel better?"

He placed another greasy kiss on my mouth. "Who do I talk to from your side who'll tell me your secrets?"

I kissed him back as I considered what he was asking. Who could he talk to? Should I invite Liam over for dinner? Introduce him to my boss? Janine who'd never break confidentiality?

I snapped my fingers. "I know how you'll find it. All my secrets."

"I don't need all of them." His expression changed, turned a little serious. "Hey, I was kidding about the secrets. You don't need to tell me anything you don't want to."

"No, there's something to it. We're both trying to start over, but we can't. We're not allowed to. There's always going to be someone in our past who knows the ugly thing we were trying to hide. We don't see it every day now because we've run away from those people, but we didn't run away far enough. They're around."

"Start over." Gio said it slowly. "Sounds good. Sounds impossible."

"But we're trying to anyway."

He shrugged. "I don't mind doing difficult things."

"Maybe there's another way to start over, Gio. Maybe it's not running away from the thing."

Own what shamed you.

Maybe if I ran right for it, took it by the horns, and stabbed it right in the heart.

MY PLACE, my bed, a different kind of threesome.

Him, me, and my phone.

I didn't delete anything. At first it was out of a stubborn insistence that I was fine, so while I set all my social media to private, I didn't delete anything. I pulled up a photo from a little over two years ago. A photo of me and my friend Bessy, two days before Bradley broke the news to me.

Bessy invited me to coffee after work to catch up. I was a little tense in that photo because while Bessy was her usual fun self, her topic of conversation was when Bradley and I would decide to get married already. I held my tongue, didn't tell her that it wasn't the right time to talk about it. The barista snapped this photo after we asked her to.

"You look—"

I watched his face as he tried to find the word.

Gio ended the mental search, his shoulders moving in a defeated shrug. "The same."

"This is Iris, before The Incident," I said. "I think the biggest problem I had at the time was paying my credit card bill, and how annoying it was that the office printer always broke down whenever I had a presentation the next day."

"Legit problems."

"I wish I cared about those again," I said, laughing a little. "You know that feeling when you look at your credit card bill and it's the day after the due and you haven't paid yet? God, I used to think that was the worst."

"It's not the worst."

"No. But you've probably never been late on a credit card bill."

"I don't have a credit card."

I rolled my eyes. "Anyway. My other most important problem at the time was that I felt that Bradley and I were growing apart. And then Bessy here suggests we should get married already, and I was twenty-two and starting to enjoy my job and..."

Well, enough of that. Moving on.

"There's a gap of like three weeks, before I even posted anything new," I told him, showing him the feed. "That's when it happened."

He pointed to the first photo of the new era, After The Incident. A sunrise with no caption. I had forgotten that I had taken that.

"I went to stay at a hotel. Bradley joined me the next day but I spent one night on my own and I went up to the roof when I couldn't sleep. I napped on a couch up there and woke up when the sun came up."

"Was it the sign you were waiting for?"

"Oh I wanted it to be. I wanted it to mean something. But it really was just the beginning."

I switched to my email app, and showed him a forward from Liam. It was an "open letter" of sorts from Tita Ara to my other family members. Typical of the extended family's childless matriarch, it was about her—her disappointment, her dismay, her shame—and then she went on to admonish the other family members for how they've raised their children to be sinful, shameful, immoral whores.

Not in those words. Something like it.

"This is intense," Gio said, flinching, but not looking away. "How did your parents even—? Your aunt took them down in front of everyone."

"Oh, my parents apologized to her. So much." I didn't know what Tita Ara did to inspire that kind of devotion from the people who spawned me, but it was obvious which side they chose. "There are other emails and posts, but this is the worst of it."

I typed a search word and showed him *all* the archived email that was about it. Thirty-eight, all forwarded by Liam, because I wasn't in the loop of course. I suspected there were more that my brother hid from me.

"You got calls when your photos went public," I reminded him. "Me? No one called. No one texted. Just Bradley and Liam, for a long time. It's like everyone else was afraid to send me a message because it would wind up in public."

"I can't believe they'd do this to you," he said, nearly a whisper. "They're your family."

"Your family has experience with scandal. Mine doesn't."

"Yeah but...shit."

Then I showed him the Facebook post, the one that outed my name as the person who had previously only been "amateur Asian hottie." Written of course by Tita Ara, and on the surface not about me, but about how this made her "think more about how we are raising our children" and how "blessed" she felt that she was now "stronger for having gone through this trial."

"What the fuck," Gio said.

"What I said, exactly."

"This was when your name went out?"

"To people who had never seen the video, yes."

"That's fucked up. I don't even know what to say."

"I'll accept 'fucked up.' It really was."

But we weren't done yet.

We had to switch to the browser so I could show him the rest of it. It was easy to find, because I had it bookmarked. The original video submission was still there; Bradley was never able to get the site to take it down, despite reporting the user who posted it. I scrolled down to the comments, and showed my new guy what everyone said about me having sex with another guy.

He flinched again, but of course, couldn't look away. That was kind of the point—you can't look away when it's there. It was the most private thing I'd ever done, the kind of thing that shouldn't be seen by people, but when people saw and started saying things, I couldn't *not* look at what they said.

she's hot
i'd do her
luv asians
i'd last longer than him, baby

"Iris..." He had taken over the phone and was scrolling down the comments himself. "I mean, shit. Yeah."

A lot of comments.

I switched to an archived Facebook post where one version of the video had been posted. The original had since been deleted, but I kept screenshots of it when it was still active.

Comments. This time not so complimentary of my hotness, and instead were remarkably similar to my aunt's condemnation of me as the worst thing to have come out of her family tree.

"How did you feel when you saw this?" he asked.

"It's weird," I said, "because it's me. They're talking about me. It's awful and I wish they wouldn't do that, but I got numb after a while."

"You mean that?"

"Yeah. Because it's all dumb stuff, and if it's not dumb, it's plain lies. Like this one." I showed him a comment of someone claiming to have been a high school classmate. "I don't have any freaking idea who she is, and she's saying I slept with her ex. Please."

"I had some of that. Well, my brother told me. He asked if there had been others, because some people were implying that there were, and if we needed to lawyer up."

"Oh my god."

"It's not true."

"Oh, I wasn't going to ask you to prove it."

He looked relieved. "Okay. I wasn't sure. I can't believe you even read this stuff about you."

It surprised me too, how strong my tolerance was for it. "You know how we all deal in different ways? It actually got easier to get it over when I read the worst. Even when they were total lies. It just put everything in perspective, that none of these people really know me or can hurt me. It's all useless words. I was talking to Janine—my therapist—about this and we sort of came to the conclusion that eventually, it all becomes the past. Everything, part of us. The best things that happened to us, and also the worst things. The way that people sometimes forget the best things about us, they'll also forget the worst. Or remember. I began to accept that. But it's hard to find people who'll be okay with it."

"I wish I could tell you that it's going to be fine," Gio said. "I probably would have, if I didn't go through what I did."

"That's all right. I don't believe anyone else when they tell me that, anyway. Even if it's true."

"Right."

I began scrolling up. Back to the video. Gio tensed and nearly let go of the phone.

"We don't have to," he said.

I squinted at him. "I don't know, Gio. This is the last thing. And I've seen your photos."

"This is different. Right? It's different. It's not fair."

"We have to talk about whether you should watch this or not."

"Why is it important to you?"

"Because it's out there. I assume that anyone who meets me has seen it."

"I haven't."

"I saw your photos."

"How many?"

There was a site that had "everything," at least ten. "A bunch. Not blurred. Pretty sure you're being blown in one of them."

"Shit." He had to have known that photo, apart from having been there in person. "But they're just photos. Could have been staged. That's how I worked it out in my head...that they can look at it all they want but the angle's always going to be off, and I could always say it was never me. If I had to. But yours is different."

Because mine was clearly me, clearly my ex-boyfriend, clearly enjoying ourselves.

"So I win this round?" I told him.

Gio was not amused. "This sucks. I hate that you had to go through this."

"Look," I said. "As far as I'm concerned, this is all my shame. All my dirt. No one can hurt me any more than I've already been hurt. If you watch it, you'll be just like the—" I checked the view count for the video. "Thirty thousand other people who watched it."

"I could still hurt you for some other reason," he said.

"But not for this." I lifted my legs off the bed. "I'm going to the bathroom. I'm leaving my phone here. You can watch it, or not watch it. When I come out, I'm just going to assume that you did. You can decide to leave and I'll be okay. Excuse me."

HOLY SHIT.

Could not believe I just did that.

Could not believe I went from wondering how to hide my Incident from my next relationship to shoving all of it in my prospect's face.

I would be so bad at card games.

I might be really bad at relationships.

Freshening up wouldn't give Gio enough time to do whatever. So I took my clothes off and stepped into the shower, and had a long one. Two hair treatment sessions later, both times actually waiting the three minutes the container said I should after applying to my hair and scalp, I rinsed and dried off, but still felt that I hadn't given him enough time.

How much time did one need to do this? Uncharted territory.

I wrapped my towel around myself. My bathroom was out in the common living space, the way my apartment was laid out. So I stepped out of the bathroom into the living room, and had to endure the few steps that brought me back to the bedroom.

Gio was sitting up, on the corner of my bed that was closest to the door.

The phone was further up on the bed.

Well, he was still here.

He looked up at me, and I looked at him.

And then it didn't matter to me anymore what he did, if this was him about to tell me goodbye, because I knew that he couldn't use that information to hurt me.

"Hey," I said.

Gio's eyes demanded my attention, and I couldn't look

away. I felt lighter, strangely enough, happier even, but it felt odd that he'd see it in my face. It felt inappropriate, like I should be somber and serious, especially if this was a breakup hurtling toward me.

"You," Gio said, "are brave and beautiful. Probably the bravest and most beautiful person I know."

That sounded wonderful. The words tickled my ears, brought a smile to my face, even as I willed my lips to stiffen, straighten. "But?"

"But nothing. There's nothing. I don't deserve to be with someone like you."

"You don't get to say that," I said. "I get to decide."

"Are you sure?"

"I am."

"When you said you wanted to start over—look, I want that too."

"I think we're doing an okay job at it so far."

"You think?" He turned slightly toward my phone on the bed, sort of glared at it like it was an intruder.

"Well, I enjoyed our second date very much."

"I should have asked you out properly today."

"Yeah," I added. "This third date could have gone better."

I couldn't help it; the smile was full on now, my brow raised, my tone sufficiently cheeky. He wouldn't have been able to resist that kind of challenge, would he?

He couldn't. "It's not done yet," he said. "And I haven't done what I want to do on a third date."

"You should give me a detailed schedule."

"It's better if I just show you."

FOURTEEN

Later, I was sprawled on my own bed, gasping, the sheets against my back damp and probably from sweat, canceling out the shower I'd just had.

"Ready?" Gio had the gall to say, sliding up beside me. He'd taken off his clothes and folded them up, piling them neatly on top of my dresser. I would have made a joke about it except that I was sensitive everywhere and no, I wouldn't be ready for anything for some time.

"No, are you kidding me," I laughed, turning to my side, turning away from the hard tip that was poking my thigh, totally ready. "Give me a minute."

"I'm happy you're happy."

"I bet you are." My body was still buzzing, happily recovering from the climax he wrung out of me with his mouth and fingers. Holy shit. It wasn't my favorite sex thing, because it took me and Bradley too long to figure out what worked for me. It could have been me not knowing how to ask for what I needed, or Bradley not taking instructions very well. You'd think we'd get it right but it still took years, and even then, each time was frustratingly inconsistent—too long to get there, wrong spot, not enough tongue pressure, or too much.

So when Gio insisted on doing this for me I was prepared for the potential of awesome, and also for what would probably be a disappointment thirty seconds later.

Except *it wasn't*.

He snuggled into me, spooning, and pushed the damp hair from my neck so he could plant a kiss there.

"I see what you did there," I said, my breaths still short. "I could feel you calibrating. Adjusting."

"I'm learning."

"You're a fast learner then."

"I told you."

"How could you have even known stuff? I could barely tell you what to do."

His forearm moved against my belly. "You squeeze when you want it faster or harder."

"What?"

"Yeah. You probably pulled out chunks of my hair. And you release when it's too much."

"You're kidding me."

"You tell me. Was just responding to the cues. Was I right?"

I could barely remember what I was saying or doing at the end of it, but how could I argue with the results? It wasn't half an hour of squirming away from an invading tongue. It felt like...being made love to.

No, really.

Endorphins had my brain.

"It's too hot in here," I muttered.

"It's fine."

"You don't think it's too hot?"

"It's definitely the hottest I've had."

"We're not talking about the same thing."

I felt a kiss against my shoulder, then my back. The feeling was new; those parts of me didn't recognize him yet. I wondered how I felt to him, if I was different somehow. Because while I loved my ex when I was with him, sex wasn't always "magical." Sometimes it was routine, unsatisfying, a lackluster new episode after an awesome midseason finale. Not that it was bad, or that I didn't like any of it. But not always fireworks, you know?

And now as the last of the fireworks were fading in my head, I wondered how I could be good for him.

I mean, not *in life* or anything profound like that. Right now. Right here, the same way that his every little affirmation made me feel like the most beautiful damn person in the world. I flashed back to how he looked on our "second date," seeing him come, feeling that release on my body.

"Oh my god," I sucked in my breath and reached behind me, touched his bare leg. "Now. You ready?"

"One second." He needed a little more than that but even a second was annoyingly long, it was like forever before he got the condom on, handled me by the hip, and pushed into me, from behind, still spooning.

Fuck, he was ambitious. This wasn't the most fun for me either, because the variables made things more difficult —lack of eye contact, clit stimulation, and, well, size and length was a factor to pulling this off.

But he had the size and the length.

"Talk to me," he said, after a shallow thrust that merely teased. That wasn't a bad first try; I wouldn't have thought a full and hard stroke would be welcome. But inconsistent arousal was inconsistent, and my body demanded more and harder despite already having more than enough.

I brought his hand to my clit and touched myself, touched myself with his fingers. "Please."

"How?"

"Faster. Harder. Everything."

"But you said you weren't ready."

"I am. I am now. I'm ready if you are."

"Fuck." His hips moved, all that power waiting only for my permission. And suddenly the whole idea of making this good for him seemed useless because I must have been getting the better end of this deal. His strokes were perfect and my clit was throbbing and I was coming all over again so soon.

I knew he'd come because I felt that tension in his hands, felt him grow rigid behind me, heard him grunt against my shoulder. He was still inside me but I told myself not to freak out; I was updated on my pill, it wasn't a fertile time of the month, he was wearing protection. He pulled out slick and smooth.

"Everything okay there?" I asked.

"Yeah. Condom didn't break."

I was thinking about whether or not to shower again when he joined me back on the bed. I was thinking of asking him if he wanted to join me. But then I didn't feel like doing anything but breathe, breathe in the scent of him, and this was how I fell asleep.

FLEXIBLE WORK HOURS and no morning meetings meant I didn't panic when I woke up at ten o'clock on a Tuesday and saw him still there beside me. The room was too cold; I slept to the same level of air-conditioning every night, but usually with more clothes on. We had somehow drifted off to opposite ends of the bed, touching only by the toes. I had the entire blanket.

"Hey."

His head had been facing the other way too. He turned it toward me, opening his eyes just barely. "You have to go?"

"I've got another hour."

"Hmm."

Gio was sleeping on his stomach and he stretched out, lazily, closing his eyes again. The muscles of his back moved as he searched for the right position to make him comfortable. Muscles that dipped and then rose up again into that bare butt, that I now shamelessly looked at.

"Cute," I said aloud, apparently.

"Hmrmhmm."

"I'm going to need to get ready for work in a bit."

"Mrrrhmmmmm."

He didn't move from that spot as I got ready to go to work. And when I left, I told him to lock up before he went back to 9J.

So my state of mind as I got into the office on Tuesday: *I have a lover*.

This was the state of mind that got me through a potentially stressful turnover session with Miley, who was serious about having me step up and represent the office in meetings with schools and donors again. As she handed me printouts and updated me on the new dean of this school and the new aid agency that pledged this much, instead of my stomach churning and figuring out how to worm my way out of it, I nodded, and took notes, and didn't at all disagree with anything she said. Even when what she was telling me was that my work life was going to drastically change and in the exact opposite of the way I had been doing it for the past two years.

No big deal.

I had a lover. Not that it made it easier, but nothing took my mind off this better than thinking about sex. Several times an hour.

"Got it?" Miley asked, something she did out of habit, and had now become my cue to look at my notes and look serious and nod.

"Yeah," I said.

"Then you're ready to join me at the meeting later."

"Oh. That's today?" I checked the calendar she had laid out on her desk, and there it was, a meeting with a partner funding foundation, a semi-annual thing that I stopped attending.

Since I didn't exactly respond with pep, Miley's brow immediately registered a frown. "Do we need to talk about this some more?"

"No." I was quick to correct my lack of pep, and maybe overdid it. "I'm sorry. It's been a while, that's all."

"We're going to talk about this anyway. Do you feel that I'm pushing you?"

"You don't think I'm drastically underqualified for this?"

"You're twenty-four, aren't you?"

"Yeah."

Miley smoothed her hair from where it started near her temple, and down to the ends near her shoulders, where they curled up a bit. Another thing she did, usually when she was about to begin a presentation or a speech. She was about to "speech" me. "I still remember being twenty-four. That was when Carl and I began planning what we'd want to do for the rest of our lives, and that led to us starting this. I also know that no one else thought I was old enough to do anything worthwhile, when I was twenty-four. I want to believe that you can take over because you've been doing so much of the work, and all you need to do next is start talking to people. Are we on the same page on that?"

"Yes," I said. "Yes I understand that."

"So the only reason this won't work, really, is if you don't want to do it. Which I told you, I'll understand, if you're impatient and want a change."

"But won't your dad have a problem with..."

"My dad, as I said, doesn't care so much about who runs this when I'm not around, as long as it doesn't lose him money."

"He's not concerned about the reputational risk?"

First of all, it was horrible that I even had to learn that term—"reputational risk." But now it was part of my vocabulary. It was part of Miley's too, and she always went tense when I used it. She was that for a second, and then she relaxed and even laughed a bit.

"I'm going to tell you something about my dad, and anyone else you'll be working with who has some influence over your future," she said. "When they've made up their mind about you, good luck trying to convince them of anything else. That's when you pack up and look for other people to have influence over your future. While they *haven't* made up their minds though, you be exactly what you want to be and work how you want to work."

"You think he hasn't made up his mind about me?"

"I think he doesn't care until you prove that you can't handle this."

"You could also hire someone else."

"Someone with experience to do this. You know how much it would cost us to replace me?"

"So I'm cheaper to keep around and keep the lights on."

"Now you see how my dad will see it. But that's not

how you'll work, won't you? I'm counting on you to keep it going, and I'll make sure you get paid right."

Too young, too inexperienced, too reputationally damaged. I was giving myself those labels; Miley wasn't. Still, she and her brother had let me work under a rock when I wanted to work under a rock, but life had to go on.

"Let's do this," I said. "Let's get more money today."

FIFTEEN

I'd been ignoring Liam's texts all this time, and the only reason I picked up when he called was I was distracted. My first day back as a people-person at work was a little rough on me, and when I got home and knocked on Gio's door, there was no answer. No message was left for me at the lobby either, and I had trekked to Tower 2 to see if he was doing his other hobby.

Then Liam called and I actually picked up.

"You're alive," he said.

"Of course I am."

"Can you not try to disappear on me? It's freaking me out."

"It's not you, you know that."

"It feels like it is."

Because he insisted on staying with the family, and insisted on trying to bring me back. "Only because of the company you keep."

"I can't believe how stubborn you're being about this. It's been a long time."

"They're doing it to me. I'm not doing anything to them."

"Iris. Iris. You can't make the first move on this? Mom misses you. She was asking how you are, and I'd know that if you actually replied to my texts."

"If she misses me then good."

"I wish you weren't doing this."

"I don't know what else to tell you. I'm not going back there. Why does it mean so much to you?"

Liam was quiet, too quiet, and I had to check to see if the call was still connected. It was.

"I didn't think it would be you," he said.

Oh.

Liam craved that kind of belonging. His own personal crisis came to a head when we were teenagers, and it took years for him to feel more comfortable in the family again. That didn't mean he got to apply his own life lessons to mine, no matter how much I loved and admired him.

It wasn't the same.

"I can talk to you on the phone," I said, stepping back from the lobby and heading out to the garden. "Do you want to know what I've been up to lately?"

"Fine. Everything okay with you?"

"I got promoted."

"No kidding."

"Yeah. And...I'm seeing someone."

"No shit!"

"Yes. Finally."

"Do I know him?"

Given Liam's social circle, he probably did. "He's great, is all you need to know."

"He treating you right?"

"Amazingly."

"Will you be introducing us?"

"Let's not go there yet."

"Come on, I miss double-dating with you."

"One of these days."

"This weekend."

"No."

"Next weekend."

"No."

"You know I won't stop."

My throat felt like it was seizing, but I let some words out. "Next weekend then."

"Friday?"

"Saturday."

"Deal."

"Who are you even taking on this date?"

"I'll find someone. Can't wait to see you, Little Flower."

"Goodbye, Liam."

The reception desk at the lobbies of the different NV Park towers had a CCTV station, a monitor that showed various feeds from within the building. I smiled at the Tower 2 guard and peered over the desk at the monitor. And that was how I found Gio, working on the puzzle. For a few seconds I just watched him, the angle of the camera showing me the top of his head, looking down as he sorted through pieces. And then I shook myself out of it, realizing that I was watching him without him knowing it.

Even off the grid, he couldn't completely escape being looked at.

"YOU CAN'T BE sure of that."

"Of course I can't. It's not like I can ask him. Or if he'd ever admit it."

"What did you do?"

I shuddered, thinking of my meeting with one of the donor foundations earlier. From the Figueras Family Foundation standpoint it went extremely well—donor reps were happy with the budget, the use of the funding, the scholar update, and pledged more money for the grant. I got to speak, answer questions, explain a disbursement schedule, without embarrassing myself or my boss.

Except for that one guy in the panel, who looked at me *that way*.

"Nothing," I told Gio. "Of course."

"Did he talk to you?"

"No. He said something, but it wasn't really at me. It's one of those things. It won't show up in a transcript or even in a video, you know? I could feel it though."

I felt his eyes on me, and the glint of recognition, knew the strange place that his memory took him even as he kept a professional distance in that room. He didn't do anything unwelcome; didn't even shake my hand.

"That sucks." Gio scooted a little closer to me. We were sitting in a booth at a pub in NV Park, drinking our dark beers, and what he did had the effect of hiding me a little from the rest of the room. "Are you going to tell your boss about it?"

"I don't know yet. I probably won't. I mean, I was so into the promotion this morning." I couldn't take back all the pep.

"You can't work in an environment where you get that kind of treatment."

"Where won't I possibly randomly encounter someone who's seen it, Gio?"

He paused and laughed. "A convent."

"A remote island."

"You'll fish for a living."

"Thanks, Gio. That's exactly the career I was looking for." I didn't particularly like having to go into isolation either. I mean, I didn't even stop the alerts to my email. "Am I being paranoid?"

"Of course not," he said. "If you think the person knows, he knows."

"How do you experience it?"

Gio knocked our beer bottles together. "I know that look too. I'm used to being recognized by random people because of when I was with Les. But after the pics, yeah. There's something else to the look, sometimes."

"Like how?"

"Look, this actually happened, so I don't think I'm making it up. I tried to date someone after. I went out with some friends, was introduced to their girl friends, and started talking to this girl who seemed interested. She looked at me that way, and later—well, she was physical really quickly."

"Wow." On two levels. Wow because yeah, I could really see that happening. If it wasn't the eyes, it was going to be the smirk, the way his voice rumbled in his throat, that perky backside, and I'd understand if someone wanted to jump him on the spot. The other level was that I'd never actually talked about this with a guy I was dating. I mean, Bradley and I talked about attractive people sometimes, as observers, but we both lacked any kind of experience with other people for the conversation to be interesting.

This was interesting.

"Yeah. I met her that night and she wanted a hookup then and there. She didn't even say anything. We were talking about something else, and then she pulled me to a room, and started kissing and touching me. And I told her to stop and asked her what was going on."

"Wow."

"But she actually did stop and talk to me about it. She'd been sending that kind of signal all night and thought I was reciprocating. I apologized and said I wasn't, and then we sort of shook hands and she left."

"That turned out well. Did it?"

"Did it? I can't tell. But that was when I learned that I could be walking and talking and doing normal shit and I was sending manwhore signals."

"Oh. That bothers you?"

"Yeah it does. I don't think I can say it's the same thing you feel when people look at you, but I worry about it."

"Do you ever feel threatened by the stranger, what they think of you?"

"I had a meeting with the family lawyer about what to do if someone ever used this for blackmail or extortion, and that scared the shit out of me. They said if I were responsible, I'd need to evaluate the extortion factor before I pursue another relationship."

"Well that's enough to make a guy go off the grid."

"I know, right? Do you feel safe where you are?"

"Yes," I said, nodding slowly. "Yes, that's why I live here, and work there. I feel safer. But I know that I can't hide from even the weird feelings. I need to win, you know? I can't let the perv looks defeat me."

"They're just looks, right? No one has actually said anything stupid? Propositioned you?"

"No."

"Okay then. One day at a time. You should tell your boss though, if anyone crosses the line."

"Of course. I mean, I like working there. I totally believe in what we're doing."

"You have a brochure for me to look at? Because yeah, I mean, I might want to find out how to get a chemistry grant going."

"I have one in my place maybe, but everything's on the website, you know. So easy if you had internet."

He gave me that smirk, and it was boyish and annoyingly adorable. "Nah, not there yet."

"I thought getting stuck in the elevator without any way to contact the world got you over that."

"But you saved me, so I'm fine."

I could tell Liam this story. I was seeing someone, and we were dating in a time warp, stuck somewhere before the year 2000, or whenever people didn't have phones glued to their hands. I wasn't bothered by any of this, by the way. If Gio wanted to be that guy, I'd let him be that.

I would let him be whoever he really was.

And that led to: "Would you have hooked up with the girl?"

"What?"

"Would you have?"

He did not expect to be asked that. "No—no I think I wouldn't."

"Because you were coming out of a long-term relationship and considered yourself a good guy. We're taught to respect people and not sleep with them the day we meet them. Of course you wouldn't. But did you want to?"

Do you like watching yourself, Iris?
What do you want, Gio?

I cleared my throat and struggled to find the words. "What I'm trying to get at is, well, you and I, we seem to like sex."

"Yeah…"

"Not only with each other. I mean, in general. We seem to like it a little more than the other people who just lie down and take it, don't you think? And don't panic."

"I'm trying not to."

"All right. But do you agree? It's not about being in love and in a relationship. We like sex and in a way that we can't really talk about with other people. Because it's not proper to talk about this with most people."

Those blue eyes darted, but he was with me.

"All I'm saying is that you can talk about it with me, okay?" I added. "If there's anything you want us to try, you should be able to tell me. In case you were thinking you couldn't. In case you think I need to be protected from that."

Our mouths met; the kiss was sweet, like a thank-you from him.

"All right," he said.

"I hope that means I can talk about it with you too."

"Anything. Anything you want. It's only fair."

"I think we should head back to your place," I said. "I've talked about work enough. Tell me about yours."

SIXTEEN

Viscosity is how thick and sticky a semifluid thing is. I know this now. I know this because I was sitting cross-legged on my couch, facing Gio, asking him to explain chemistry, and cosmetics, how one decides to get a degree in chemical engineering when the family business was going to keep him wealthy anyway.

"Because I don't like them," he said matter-of-factly.

"I don't like my family either," I told him.

There were differences in our runaway situations though. I preferred that we talk about the chemistry. He lit up in a totally different way, whenever I asked him about it.

"...at the time that I came in, they had just started the in-house manufacturing and wanted an 'all-natural' line..."

"...Manolo's been working there for years but in marketing and with the import subsidiary; he can't be bothered to attend the seminars and conferences he'd need for anything regulatory, and I was into this anyway..."

"...I know they had to work on this a lot because we weren't sure about the dry rate, never worked with this kind of film before..."

It didn't take much to let him continue at this, and before we knew it, it was an hour of pigments, adherence, formulation, long wear.

"You're not bored?"

"Are you kidding? You're good at this."

"But you work where you work and you're interested. No one else I know is interested in this."

No one else asked an attractive blue-eyed boy to explain viscosity to them. And why not? Why hadn't anyone else ever wondered why lipstick felt the way it did, when it slid across her lips?

I uncrossed my legs and rose up on my knees. Between us was Bella Mariel lipstick 843, yet to be given a sassy feminine name, and I popped the cap off the tube, twisted it to push up the bullet-shaped product inside. It was a darker red, something I probably would have chosen for myself, something I'd wear on a night out, when I still did that. It was a subtle red though, because as Gio explained, you couldn't use some pigments if you were going for certain types of certification. Certainly not the kind of red that's obtained from crushed insects.

Placing one hand on his knee to steady myself, I brought the tube to my mouth and applied 843, bottom lip first, generously, then swept through my upper lip twice, imagining myself in front of a mirror. The lipstick felt creamy and smooth, welcome because I was always a drink away from feeling chapped. It smelled...fruity. There was something mildly cool about it too.

"Is there mint in this?" I asked.

Gio straightened up and it was a shorter distance now to my mouth and he kissed me, tasted it for himself. I didn't allow him a light peck though; I made sure the kiss lingered, and he got to taste lipstick, and lips, and tongue.

He pulled away and laughed softly. "Yes. I can confirm mint."

His lips and the side of his mouth were streaked with it now. "You're right, this thing doesn't adhere very well."

Gio began the adorable and futile task of rubbing lip color off his face without knowing where exactly it was, and I swatted his hands away to do it myself. The red on his face was a map of my favorite nibbles, apparently, from the smear on his lower lip and right underneath it, the corner of his mouth, a spot on his jaw halfway to his chin. Rubbing it off with my thumb wasn't working; all it did was spread it around, thinly, like a modest blush on the lower part of his face.

"Let me guess," I said, "something to do with the solvent?"

"It's meant to stay on skin," Gio said through a smile. "There's some level of resistance to natural skin oils and sweat."

"Great. This'll have to stay on you for a while."

"You know what it doesn't have as much resistance against?"

"What?"

"Saliva."

"I think I have a delivery device for that," I said, and I started with the corner of his mouth, the one I inexplicably liked.

―――

IF LIPSTICK WAS all over his face then it had to have been all over mine too, but he didn't say anything about it, didn't pause to have me wash up. Those precious minutes were instead spent getting naked, getting ready, getting safe, getting inside me. We hadn't even moved to the bed, and were still on my couch, figuring out how to do missionary on the cramped space.

But we figured it out.

What I liked about him being on top was I got to watch him. Watched the tension in his arms, his shoulders, the way his hips, his torso, his entire body worked for his pleasure and mine. It was hot, and one of the best ways to cap an hour-long discussion on chemistry, in my humble opinion.

"Which date are we on now?" I struggled to ask. "What are we supposed to be doing?"

"I don't even remember," he admitted, distracted by his own thrusting. "I don't care. Exactly what this is."

My legs wrapped around his waist, bringing himself closer, tightening the connection between us. I pushed his shoulders back so I'd still get a view, still get to see the effect of our joining on my body.

I wasn't even sure when I came. At some point I had closed my eyes and lost sense of time, and missed several beats, missed seeing the exact moment when he climaxed so the rest of my senses had to make up for it. Heard it, felt it.

His weight on top of me, as he recovered, was a comfortable kind of heavy.

Anchored, more than suffocated.

"You're everything," Gio said. "You're intelligent and you care and you listen to people. You're everything."

It was sudden and it surprised me, and I could do nothing but blink at him. He lifted his head, kissed my forehead.

SEVENTEEN

"No lunch today, unfortunately," Matilda told me, when we saw each other at the pool that Saturday. "Everyone else is busy."

"No problem," I said, adjusting my bikini top as I waded in from the shallow end. "I'm hanging out with Gio later anyway."

"That's great." Matilda slipped her sunglasses on and it looked like she was back to tanning and sipping a fruit shake in a white takeout cup at the same time. I dipped into the water and did a lap. When I surfaced, she was sitting back up again, looking at me.

"You two are okay, right?" she asked me. "You and Gio."

"We're awesome."

"I'm glad."

"What are you worried about?"

"Just that you two had your fifteen minutes of shame, and it might make other people think they have the right to...comment."

I raised an eyebrow at her. "It wasn't just fifteen minutes."

"You know what I mean."

"But thank you for trying very hard not to comment."

"It's none of my business. But you're my friend now, and I protect my friends."

"Is there something I need protecting from?"

Matilda's laugh came out like a snort. "The world in general?"

"That's a lot of enemies." It did feel that way sometimes, and I was glad that someone else understood. I was glad that the guy I was seeing also understood. Maybe this was what Janine was describing, when she said I deserved to be around people who got me. I didn't think it was going to be soon, or at all possible, without compromising.

"The ignorant and judgmental aren't even worth elevating to the level of enemy," she said. "But anyway. My friends tell me I'm the fighting sort. I keep acting like I have something to prove. You don't have to. But yeah, I'm here for you."

I gave her a thumbs up and continued with another lap. Matilda's philosophy, I could see, was justice. She had something taken away from her, and she needed to get it back on her own terms, so she would feel closure.

Sometimes I wished that I could be that person that no one singled out, that no one used as an example or a cautionary tale.

Good luck.

We could only move forward.

SO, Saturday football. The way Gio mentioned it, it was like kids kicking a ball at the empty lot down the street. Which was technically true—but "empty lot" was a fenced outdoor field with artificial turf, "down the street" was within the NV Park complex, and "kids" were athletic guys and girls in their twenties, everyone seemingly above average in terms of attractiveness.

He didn't ask me to sit through the entire thing. In fact, the specific instructions were to "pick him up," sometime after five, and possibly catch the end of this Saturday football game. I approached the fence carefully, looking for the entrance, and saw a portion that opened like a door.

I recognized some of the people from the different NV Park towers. I figured that people who lived here would be using the field, or form some kind of league, but they didn't have uniforms.

Like, that guy who looked like he was from Tower 3 like us, he was in white. And another guy was in blue. Both of them seemed to be teammates with Gio, in red. Good thing they knew what they were doing and weren't confused by the lack of labeling.

This is so college, I thought again, not the first time as I reflected on this thing with Gio. Bradley was in the music org, and more than once I waited outside the meeting room for him to be done with whatever assembly. He did the same for me, that semester I took a late afternoon tennis PE class.

Like I'm dating the football star.

I spotted him, my guy among the other players. Sweaty, his shirt smeared with a diagonal of dirt. If the experience hanging out with him in the daytime was new, so was this one, seeing him with people. We were too proud of being self-identified runaways; I took for granted that he could be among people and function.

Did he see me the same way?

Later, I met the football gang. Damon, Andrea, and

Ethan. I smiled and shook their hands, and braced my "perv detector" senses. These were Gio's friends, and yeah, they probably knew who I was, and what had happened. It was always better to assume anyone new I met had seen the video; my nerves were steeled and ready.

"Ethan's the guy I know from college and the Eng org," Gio said. "He had 9J before me."

"Oh, cool," I said. "It's a nice place. But you're still in the building?"

"I live with my girlfriend," Ethan replied. "In 10J."

"Right above?" said I, Captain Obvious.

"I know," Gio said, rolling his eyes. His friends did variations on laughing and smiling at Gio's exaggerated annoyance, and oh, this was an old joke.

His friends *joked* about being in the room underneath the one your friend is probably having sex in. It took me a beat to decide if I was going to be uncomfortable with this—and I wasn't.

"Nice to meet you, Iris," Andrea said, and she was fixing her bag while she said it so I didn't notice how she was looking at me. "Want to join us for dinner? We're going to the katsu place in the new building."

All eyes, including the blue ones, landed on me.

"Actually, I haven't asked Iris where she wants to go," Gio said. "Give us a sec."

"You haven't asked her because you don't have a phone," Andrea snarked. "You can't leave messages in bottles when you're dating someone, Mella."

"Do you want katsu, Iris?" Gio asked.

"The unlimited salad makes it all worth it," Andrea added.

Did I want katsu, was also: did I want to know his friends. Did I want to be part of this group. Did I want to be part of his social circle, any kind of social circle, where we'd have to be somewhat public about being together.

"Yes," I said. "Katsu sounds delicious."

"I'LL PAY FOR IT."

"No you won't."

"You're not playing without a shirt," Damon insisted.

While this argument between Gio and Damon was going on, I'd been silent, savoring the breaded fried chicken goodness in my mouth, but yeah, then I needed to giggle a little. Nothing like guys taking something too seriously.

"I'm using my own damn shirt," Gio retorted.

"Don't make me look like shit," Damon was saying. "Captain can't even get all his team a shirt. I'm paying for it."

"We're using it once," Gio said. "I'm not paying for something I'll wear once."

"It's a *shirt*. Use it again two thousand times, I don't care. I'm paying for it. You're welcome."

This was circuitous, and it went on for a little too long. Andrea and Ethan were already in a side conversation about Ethan's girlfriend and where she was that day. And I was eating my katsu.

"You're okay, right?"

Suddenly Andrea was asking me something, drawing me into her side of the noise. "Me?" I thought she meant my food, which she was concerned about when we first sat down. "Yeah, this is perfect."

"No." Andrea did not mean my food, and her head bobbed in my direction. Then at Gio's, beside me, and back to me. "You two. You're seeing Gio, right?"

He was right there too, as she was saying this. "Uh, yeah."

"And you're fine? Because he's great, but the off-the-grid thing has to be annoying sometimes."

"I'm fine."

Andrea squinted at me, suspicious. "He refuses to bring a phone and spend money on anything."

"He's spent money on things."

"Oh. Good." Andrea shrugged. "I mean, it's fine if he does it to himself, but I can't sit here and watch you have to go through it, you know? It's icky."

"I'm fine," I repeated. "I can buy myself shirts, if that's what you're worried about, even if he doesn't want to."

"I shouldn't have told you about it," Damon declared, to Gio. "Should have just given you the thing."

"You can give it to me," I said, inserting myself right in there. "Gio. If you don't want the shirt, give it to me after the game. I'll keep it."

That seemed to satisfy his benefactor. "Perfect." Damon nodded at me. "It's done. You're wearing it at the game against Taylor Global."

"You play against companies in NV Park?" I asked.

"Damon's really into this," Gio explained. "If he were in charge, there would be a real league and it'd be televised."

"There would be cheerleaders," Andrea added.

"Sponsorships," Ethan said. "Maybe you wouldn't mind that, Gio."

"I'm not against money," Gio protested. "I don't like money with strings."

"It's honest money. But you have to wear a logo on your chest," Damon teased.

"It's a neighborhood league. You can't kick me out for not wearing the outfit you like, Esquibel."

Damon turned to me. "We let him hang out with us because he has principles. We need someone with principles around sometimes."

"You seem like upstanding citizens," I said.

"Law-abiding of course." Andrea was just as cheeky as her boyfriend, if not more per square inch because she was shorter. "But definitely the poster children for questionable decisions."

My cheeks burned a little at that. We hadn't talked at all about my Incident but they had to have known. They had to have known that the new addition to their table had a questionable decision or two under her belt.

"Even him?" I pointed to Ethan who looked like a good guy, and was so far quiet.

He shook his head. "Don't start with me. There's a list."

NIGHT SWIMMING WAS A BETTER option when the night wasn't cold, and that was where Gio and I ended up after dinner with his friends. We had the pool to ourselves as midnight neared, though maybe that was a temporary situation. Saturday night was busy for the pool area, and I wasn't sure if we were lucky that we chanced upon it empty, or we were just too early.

"They like giving me a hard time, but they're fun," he was telling me, pulling me to one corner of the pool.

"Did you know them before you moved here?"

"Just Ethan, and barely. I probably had three conversations with him in college. He helped out a lot as org alumni, gave career talks. He gave up a job in San Francisco for his girlfriend."

"Was that the questionable decision he made?"

"I think at the time everyone thought he was crazy."

I shrugged. "That he stayed here, or that he stayed for love?"

"He did say there was a list."

Deeper we went, and the corner he chose was the darker side of the pool, water coming up to my chest. He bent his knees and sank in, his bare shoulders just making it above the surface. It brought us face to face, eye to eye.

He had to know how I felt about those eyes.

I kissed him, teeth pulling at his bottom lip. My arms went around him and we waded further into the corner, exploring with our mouths and hands in water and in the dim light. I didn't know how nervous I'd been about meeting more of his friends until now that it was over, and I was relieved that they were—well, I wasn't sure what I'd been expecting. He spoke about his family and "that world" they lived in as if they were evil creatures, and I didn't think I'd be meeting pleasant people at all from his side.

But the NV Park friends were pleasant, and welcoming, and I didn't feel judged. I was happy for him, happy he had this support system even if he was deliberately living the way he was. How lucky for him to have stumbled upon this.

Lucky for me to have stumbled upon him?

Because for some reason what I wanted right then and there was a kiss that would make me forget my name, and he seemed to know it. Then the next thing I wanted was more, and he seemed to know that, because his hand had trailed down my back, around my hip, tracing the hem of the bottom of my bathing suit.

"Yes," I said without him asking, and he knew that I wanted his finger exactly where it went. I didn't even know how to ask for it but he knew, and good thing, because it was an amazing feeling. I didn't expect the intensity of it, and I clung to his neck, but he kept his body rigid, his breathing level, his movements all under water, unseen. But that was it, wasn't it? The possibility of being caught, seen, being watched by someone on a higher floor who just happened to look down. I felt him move slightly and another finger slide inside me and I came hard, biting my lip, feeling like I'd drawn blood.

"Oh my god," I said, catching my breath. Collecting the pieces of myself. "Oh my god."

"Yeah?"

"I wanted that and I didn't know how to say it."

He kissed my forehead. "I'm beginning to get it."

EIGHTEEN

Just when I was getting ready to wind down my work day, I got a knock on my door.

"Conference room in five minutes," my boss told me.

"I don't have anything in my calendar."

"I forgot that we had this and that you should be in it. Thirty minutes, applicant panel. Do you have other plans?"

I did, but Miley couldn't have known that. Or maybe she sensed it, because I had come in by nine a.m. and that hadn't happened in a while. On a normal day shift at work, I'd come in early and leave before six. I made plans to have dinner with Gio a little earlier than usual, because the late night everything was starting to take a toll, but I wasn't exactly going to tell him to cut down on our couple time. I liked the couple time. The couple time was very satisfying.

"Half an hour is fine," I said. "You're letting me sit in?"

"Well yeah, because you'll have to do that now."

Right. Sometimes, we conducted scholarship application interviews in the office. It wasn't an everyday thing, because if the applicant wasn't in Manila, we arranged for a video chat session instead. Sometimes the sponsor who wanted to listen in on the interview wasn't in Manila, or the Philippines, and when a conference call was planned I was silently part of it, taking notes or answering questions.

"Who's the panel?" I asked her.

"Two applicants together," she said. "And then you and me."

"Just you and me? No one sent anyone else?"

Miley nodded. "That's why I want you in there. You ready?"

I wasn't thinking about that. Instead, I mentally worked out my schedule, figured out if I'd make it to the seven-thirty p.m. plans with Gio, and came up with a plan B of calling the lobby and leaving a message with them if I definitely ran late. All while picking up my notepad, a pen, and shutting down the work laptop. By the time I entered the conference room, Miley and two female students wearing different school uniforms had taken their places around the glass oval table.

The way the interview went was no different from the others that I had joined before. Miley led this, and spoke through most of it. She introduced herself, said hello to the girls. I checked my file—Pamela and Mikayla, both in grade 11. They were two of five shortlisted students up for a premed scholarship. From the file I could tell that Pamela was a sure thing, but Mikayla was still conditional, based on the personal assessment she'd be getting after this session.

Wow. That always felt so heavy to me. We did fulfilling work here but for every one person who got good news, ten others probably would be bummed that day, or longer. Sometimes when the competition was tough, it came down to this—what you said in a room, to a person like Miley, or apparently me. It was so Ms. Universe sometimes.

Pamela was doing well at this, and I could tell that her

sure spot was well-deserved. Mikayla was less articulate but in a way that was totally understandable. She was a kid! Not a practiced pageant candidate. They were both turning seventeen, and while we'd seen some excellent young people apply and get their grants, I did still remember what I was like at that age.

I mean, look at the questionable decisions I'd made just a few years ago.

There was a list of questions that Miley was going through, and she tapped my foot, and slid her notebook over to me. She wanted me to ask the last one.

"Oh," I said. "Yeah. 'In your application, you were asked to talk about why you want to pursue a career in science and how you see your future in it. Can you tell us a little bit about that now?'"

When students applied to get a grant, they got to prepare for this question. They could do their research, write their drafts, ask for people to check their work before submitting. Miley told me that the interview was usually so she could *hear* the answer, and sometimes she'd discover in the applicant's voice if she believed her written answer for real.

Mikayla, based on her file, was from a family of English teachers and government employees. Not exactly lowest economic bracket, not exactly top of her class. But she looked at me in the eye and said, simply, "No one in my family has ever taken medicine, or worked in science. We don't know anyone who has. I said in my essay that I might be the first doctor in the family and sometimes I just hope that means I get to show my sisters that I can do this. I mean, I'm so thankful to my parents and they love me, but they can't imagine my future in this and I don't want to be stuck with whatever small dream they have."

It was simple, direct. Not exactly a tearjerker or literary winner. But damned if I didn't know exactly what she meant, and I wrote a note to myself to fight for her, if I were given the chance.

GIO WAS WAITING for me at the lobby when I arrived, indeed thirty minutes late. He had been sitting on one of the couches, and he had keys in hand.

"Where to this time?" I asked, smoothing his collar down as I kissed him.

"I know you just got back home, but is it all right if we run out for an errand before dinner? How hungry are you?"

"Not that hungry."

"This should be quick."

"You have a car?"

Gio looked sheepish. "I do, but not this one. I didn't take it with me when I moved here. This is Damon's."

Damon's car was sleek and black, but still a practical sedan type. I might have been expecting a hulking SUV, but cars were not their people, people were not their cars. It took Gio a few seconds to adjust things when he got into the driver's side, but it seemed like he'd borrowed Damon's car before.

"I'm sorry," he began, as the engine roared to life. "I'm sorry you're experiencing this version of me. I should be driving my own car. Calling you instead of leaving dumb messages."

"You had a reason to give those up when you did."

"Yeah, but conveniences exist for a reason." He talked as if he were berating himself, as we exited the NV Park complex together. "It's not fair to you to have to bear with it."

I laughed. "It's fine. It'd be nice if we didn't need so many things to get by."

"Right? Like right now, this errand. I'm meeting my brother because I'm borrowing clothes."

"There are clothes stores right in front of..."

"Yeah but I only need something to wear for two or three meetings with the same people. I'm not buying new clothes for that."

"You're not borrowing those from Damon either?"

He cocked an eyebrow at me and apparently the answer was no. "The guy's generous, but I'm already imposing enough. And my brother borrowed clothes from me all the time when I lived at the house, so this is payback."

"Where does your brother live?"

"BGC. But we're not going there, we're meeting him at work instead. He's got a shoot at a hotel tonight."

A few things about this errand, which were revealed to me in stages. Manolo Mella was still in the family business, but in the marketing and selling side of it. That included "work" meaning fashion magazines, blogs, anything beauty-related either to mention the cosmetics or have people use them. Sometimes this meant working nights and location shoots.

The "hotel" wasn't what I thought it would be either, when we pulled up at the place that Gio's brother Manolo had texted him to go to. I mean, I had an idea of their family and his background, so I was expecting five-star service and fancy. Instead we pulled into a dark alley and stopped underneath a motel sign advertising rates for three-hour "quickies."

We stopped right there in the driveway because he

couldn't believe where we ended up either. He'd had that look as soon as we entered the neighborhood, but this all confirmed his suspicions.

"Ah shit," he muttered. "Manolo's always such a dick."

"Explain please?"

"I couldn't go to a place like this before. Because of Les."

I leaned further out so I could see more of the sign through the windshield. I'd never been here before, but had heard of it. "I lost my virginity in a place like this," I told him. "It's kind of where it happens if you don't have your own condo and your parents never leave town."

"You think I'm judging? I'm not. I'd do the same thing if it didn't—" He shook his head and tried to start over. "I ask to borrow three shirts, two pairs of pants, and a coat from my brother. Told him I'm willing to go to his place tonight to pick it up. Or pick it up from his office at any time, because I don't have anything to do all day."

"But he makes you go to this...motel."

"Yes he does. He also has an assistant who delivers things for him. Delivers things for Kimmy. For our mother. But yeah, I ask for clothes and he makes me go to a damn motel."

"This is a joke to him?"

"Yeah, he thinks he's hilarious."

"It's not so bad," I said. "I mean, I haven't been to this place but if we're not having sex in it we should be fine."

"Let's just get this over with."

So the plan was, ironically, to get in and out. A quickie. It was easy to find a parking spot, and we laughed over how Damon would react when he found out that his car had been sitting there. The lobby was somewhat crowded with couples waiting to check in, but we didn't have to line up;

Gio mentioned that he was there for the shoot, somewhere on the fifth floor, and we were allowed to go up.

The elevator smelled like car freshener. Not the kind I liked. I sniffled noisily and Gio nudged my foot.

"Your first time was in a place like this?"

"Well, nicer than this."

"Was it good?"

I wasn't sure how to answer that, but at least the elevator doors had opened and we had to decide whether to head left or right down the hallway, so I had a few seconds to gather my thoughts. It was totally fair to talk about my first time, I decided, because we already kind of talked about his.

"It wasn't bad," I admitted. "Because we didn't give up after that weird first go. But you know that, since you did two your first time."

"Haha," he said, taking that with a smirk.

We found the room. It was easy; it was the one with indiscreet noises coming from inside. Nothing sleazy, just... noisy. People were in there, yelling instructions at each other.

So, the room. It wasn't what I was expecting to see either, despite having had to readjust my expectations like seventy times in one evening. It was a large room, larger than I'd seen in a place like this. Large bed, large widescreen TV...and a swing.

A swing, no joke. A block of wood secured to the ceiling on each end by metal chains, hovering right over a corner on the foot of the bed, and a beautiful woman dressed in red lingerie and a tiara was sitting on it. Sitting on it with one leg extended impossibly high up, so I'd notice the stiletto sandal wrapped around her foot. Some guy held a fan toward her face and it was making her hair fly in unnatural directions.

Her lipstick was also an excellent, excellent shade of dark red. Gorgeous and sinful.

"Wow," I couldn't help but say, as she turned away from me and toward the camera, that snapped as soon as she did.

"Are you supposed to be here?" someone was asking Gio.

"They're with me."

The guy in the corner, the good-looking one who spoke and was now headed toward us, had to be Gio's brother. Now that was someone who looked as expected, and more. An older version of Gio but darker eyes, darker hair, stubbly jaw instead of smooth. My brain composited a mental image of him and Kimmy together and wow, yeah, they looked good. Their relationship was probably intense.

"Here," Manolo said, handing Gio a backpack and a coat in a clear dry-cleaner bag. "And you must be Iris."

"Hi," I said.

"This is my dick brother Manolo," Gio said.

Manolo was smiling like he'd successfully pranked his brother. "Oh come on. When I found out that this was where we'd be shooting, I had to."

"Because you're a dick."

"My brother lived under a rock for many, many years." Manolo was talking to me now, still completely charming. "He didn't get to experience life the way his deviant brother did."

"Thanks for the clothes," Gio replied.

"No problem. What are they for?"

"Serious meetings with serious people."

"Are you getting a job?"

Gio headed out to the door. "We're heading out now. Thanks, bro."

"You're not answering my question."

This all sounded friendly and joking, by the way, from where I was standing. I liked bantering with my brother and could go entire hours with him without saying a word I actually meant. It was fun, and our version of sport because we weren't into actual sports. I wasn't sure yet how this was supposed to feel.

Gio sighed and turned around, to find Manolo closer to us. Gio was the leaner of the two, but it might only have been a posture thing; the difference of maybe ten years between them not seen at all in height or in build. God, what a great set of genes.

"It's not anything yet," Gio said. "Don't go announcing it."

"Hey. You know they'll need enough notice if you're not coming back."

"Can someone get her cleavage sweat?" someone yelled, and that made me look at my cleavage, and then over to the swing where the model was dabbing her chest with a paper towel.

"They can't understand why I'm not running back to *this*?" Gio was trying to shut this down but in the least dramatic way possible. Because it wasn't his way even if it might have been a family trait. "Not the place to talk about this, Manolo."

"Fine, fine." Manolo's hands went up, a gesture of surrender, and he leaned between us to open the motel room's door. "Giovanni gets to decide how to live his life. You going on Sunday?"

That was meant for Gio, and he answered, "Of course not."

"But Kimmy—"

"I said no already."

"*Fine*. Have you two had dinner?"

I shook my head, but then caught Gio's frozen face and realized that he didn't want to let that on. Whoops.

"Don't leave without trying the crispy pata," Manolo said, winking at his brother. "This place is known for that. Best in the city."

They sort of looked at each other and then dismissed each other simultaneously. Gio motioned for me to step out, and Manolo nodded at me then went back into his corner of the room. No goodbyes, nothing else. Fascinating. I watched Gio's face as we walked back to the elevator, imagining the mental scrubbing he was doing to himself, the same kind of thing I did whenever I interacted with family.

But my family wanted nothing to do with me, and his…

"What's on Sunday?" I asked.

He was fiddling with the backpack. "Family gathering."

I nodded. "I hate those."

Then we were at the lobby again, freakishly still crowded for a weekday evening, and I turned automatically back toward the parking lot, but the hand on my elbow led me past the exit and toward the…the motel's restaurant.

"You're kidding me," I squeaked. "You want to?"

"Best in the city," Gio told me. "You heard my brother. He's a dick but he knows what he's talking about."

NINETEEN

The email alerts were the worst of alarm clocks. Liam told me to turn them off, but I felt I needed them. Not the hate or the judgment, but a grip on what was real, even if I didn't like it. They were alarm clocks that got me ready for Monday morning, but didn't keep Monday from happening. Besides, the alerts were also the best way to find out when people stopped talking about me. I needed them; couldn't not have them. I needed to know when people were forgetting, moving on.

When I was called a slut for the first time, I remembered it. Very clearly, and at the time I could quote it down to the punctuation marks. A few other times I was called a name I was hurt too, but the majority of the comments, especially the unoriginal ones, they were just noise that would eventually fade away.

So when I saw the unread email alert for my name again, well. Shit.

I followed the link to a gossip blog. I wasn't namechecked on the main post, but actually a comment, dozens of comments down.

looks like iris len-larioca the one who did a video with her boyfriend, an anonymous user helpfully said, last night, at 10:34 p.m. *he likes sluts.*

When I scrolled back up all the way to the original post, only twenty-four hours old as of that morning, I saw it in context. It was a dark, blurry photo of Gio at the pub in NV Park, with someone I could certainly confirm was me.

"Is this Gio Mella's new girlfriend?"

"This," like I wasn't a person. Semantics.

I didn't have an alert for Gio's name. If I had, I would have known about this twenty-four hours ago, and...and what? What would have changed? He obviously didn't know about this, and wouldn't have known. He wouldn't have been able to tell me that my name was being dragged over fresh dirt.

"Never read the comments," is good advice for anything, but I had to. Bad habit.

i thought they'd get back together
glad they're totally broken up—he's such a bad influence!
obviously he's a perv
doesn't deserve her
sluts go with sluts

And so on.

I had work that day. Actual work. And an actual life that required bills to be paid and no, I couldn't stay home and read stupid comments all day even if I wanted to. Most of them weren't even about me, which made sense because these people only even knew Gio because of his ex. But then Mr. Anonymous recognized me and now my name was in there for everyone to see, again.

It was one blog post. Maybe it would go away. Gio and Les weren't together anymore. Surely they'd rather be talking about her and whatever else she was doing.

MORE THAN TWENTY alerts in the morning.

A dozen more by lunchtime.

Because I'd added "gio mella" to my alert list and set it to send me the notification as soon as it was found. I didn't let that interrupt my workday, and the alerts remained unread in my inbox. But they kept coming. Most of them for "gio mella" and maybe one or two for "iris len-larioca" and variations of the spelling throughout the day. Sometimes it was an alert for the same page, because it had been updated with a new comment.

Even so, this was us. I was ninety-seven percent sure that any boneheaded comments directed at Gio right now was because they had discovered who I was, and what I'd been "famous" for. If he had been photographed with the sweetest schoolteacher in the city, maybe the blogs wouldn't be burning up like this.

I wondered if I should tell him.

I wondered who to ask.

I lost my best friends after The Incident. No, not true—I'd lost them a little before then, when we all got boyfriends and sunk into that "my boyfriend is my best friend and my only friend" trap. Eventually they married their boyfriends, so now they were husbands, and they weren't that easy to grab for a panicked phone call or a long dinner discussing my latest dilemma.

"Happy weekend," my boss told me as I shut down and left at the decent hour of six p.m. "I saw that you sent out all the proposals today."

Yeah, even the ones we'd scheduled for Monday. I did that. I became a productive little worker bee whenever the internet turned against me.

"Is there a problem?" I asked.

Miley was surprised by the reaction. "No problem at all," she said. "Good job, is what I wanted to say."

That was a compliment, the kind that mattered. I wished I had been able to savor it, but instead my mind was somewhere else.

GIO WASN'T IN 9J. He wasn't doing his puzzle in Tower 2 either. With those options out, I had no idea how else to reach him. Just when I decided to maybe break it to him that he was a trending topic yet again, I couldn't find him.

Maybe that was a good thing? At least I was able to run my thoughts by someone else.

"Is that what you think you should do?"

I sighed. "I keep thinking of how I'd want it, if it were me. I'd want to know. I'd want to have a conversation."

"You think that's not what he wants?" Janine replied.

"He doesn't have a phone; that's how much he doesn't want this. That's his line, isn't it? He decided what it is and I can't cross it."

"Yet you called me."

"Yeah, I did."

"Because you obviously want to talk to him about it."

"I think someone should warn him? He's been doing new things lately. He said he's going to try to start working again and went to a meeting today. Shouldn't news that this is out affect him?"

"Iris, it seems like it's inevitable. Gio might want to try to hide, but he's not hiding deep and far enough. Based on what you've said, it looks more like he's biding his time, so he can do things on his terms and not anyone else's."

She was probably right. I bit my nails absently. "That makes sense."

"So ask me your question."

"I don't have one."

"Okay, we can do it that way, or we can cut twenty minutes out of this and talk about the thing you want to know, but aren't asking."

"God, you're so annoying sometimes."

"Tell me if this is one of those times when you need me to be annoying."

"Well, yeah. Okay. Tell me."

"Is the relationship going well?"

"Yes it is."

"What's happening that makes you not want to have the important conversation with him?"

"He's meeting my brother tomorrow."

"I see."

"And everything. Everything's happening. Everything's happening and it's...nice."

"You think the conversation will end the 'nice'?"

"Of course it will."

"You can't go by history with this. He isn't Bradley."

"The characters are different but the lesson is the same, you think?"

"What do you think the lesson was, Iris?"

My laptop screen was glowing bright, in front of me. My email inbox was loaded up and I was watching new alerts come in. Now over a hundred.

"Don't get hurt," I said. "Don't allow people to hurt you."

"Are you getting hurt right now?"

Not yet. Because I hadn't read the new hurtful words. It was almost midnight but I knew what I had to do. The conversation with Gio was not going to happen tonight.

"Maybe not," I told Janine. "Maybe the same sticks and stones can't hurt me as much anymore."

"Don't test yourself too much, Iris."

"I know."

"The next stage of your life is about freedom, didn't we agree? You get to choose what you let back in."

"I know."

"Call me when you need to talk."

"I will."

I ended the call, tossed my phone over to the table beside my bed, and prepared to dive into the inbox. Back in the cesspool.

TWENTY

Anonymous, 10:31 a.m.
 I'm so sad for Les :(
Anonymous, 10:43 a.m.
 y? she dumped his ass.

ANONYMOUS, 10:45 a.m.
 they were together long time. maybe they could reconcile.
Anonymous, 11:33 a.m.
 you insane? she deserves better.

ANONYMOUS, 10:38 a.m.
 She's hot I'd do her
Anonymous, 1:15 p.m.
 she'd probably let you

ANONYMOUS, 10:40 a.m.

well that's it. can't save him now.
Anonymous, 1:31 p.m.
Save him why?
Anonymous, 1:40 p.m.
years with les. first love. sad that it was all ruined because of sex.

ANONYMOUS, 10:52 a.m.
hs classmate of iris l. icy bitch.
Anonymous, 10:53 a.m.
she didn't like sucking your dick?
Anonymous, 2:15 p.m.
she wished
Anonymous, 2:17 p.m.
you wish loser.

ANONYMOUS, 10:57 a.m.
Hope he wakes up from the whoring and realize he had a good thing
Anonymous, 10:59 a.m.
you really want her back with an asshole like ds? he's jst going to say sorry?
Anonymous, 11:00 a.m.
love conquers all
Anonymous, 11:01 a.m.
get yourself some self-respect

ANONYMOUS, 11:11 a.m.

bye les. boy likes sluts.
Anonymous, 2:15 p.m.
do you know his family? they're all the same.
Anonymous, 2:27 p.m.
men are all the same.

ANONYMOUS, 11:35 a.m.
I give it 2 more weeks. Now that we know he likes a buffet.

ANONYMOUS, 12:15 p.m.
you judgmental hypocrites. so what if he likes sex. it's not like he stole from you or stabbed your mother. he's not a criminal
Anonymous, 3:31 p.m.
nice defense! maybe he'll fuck you too when he's done with her.

ANONYMOUS, 11:54 a.m.
My cousin went to high school with him and he was so nice then. I hope he gets over this phase.
Anonymous, 3:35 p.m.
poor you. you think he'll change? he's a man.

ANONYMOUS 11:58 A.M.
didn't like gio for les. she should be happy.

ANONYMOUS, 12:15 p.m.
pretty slut.

ANONYMOUS, 12:27 p.m.
saw her video? decent job.
Anonymous, 12:30 p.m.
you mean blow job
Anonymous, 12:37 p.m.
you mean indecent

ANONYMOUS, 12:29 p.m.
this is disgusting. keep your bedroom activities to yourselves. you should be ashamed.

AND SO ON.

This was the kind of thing that sucked me in, and before I knew it, it was Saturday afternoon and there was a knock on my door.

There Gio stood, cleaned up and good at it. I recognized the button-down shirt as one of Manolo's from when I watched him unpack it the night we picked it up. Crispy pata night. Oh god, dinner at a seedy motel night. If someone got a lot of mileage out of an innocent photo of him and me at a pub, what kind of drama would our motel dinner stir up?

Oh god, and then the thing at the pool...?

But Gio smiled at me like he was unaware that he was the object of internet vitriol, for the past two days. He looked more surprised that I still wasn't ready to go.

Right, dinner with my brother.

"Did I get the time wrong?" he asked.

There was no rush, since they were coming to NV Park to visit us and all we needed to do was cross the street, but I had been exposed to the hateful comments all night and all day and I felt that my apartment was filthy with it. I cleaned up as quickly as I could and got us out of there.

TWENTY-ONE

Liam's date was someone I actually recognized. "Jules, right?" I said as I shook his hand. From college, at least around that time, because Liam had a lot of friends who didn't go to his school. Jules was a thin, lanky guy back then, but I remembered how funny their conversations were when we were all together. Jules still looked a lot like he did before, but with an extra ten pounds and glasses, nothing about it unwelcome. He and my brother looked good together.

"You remember," Jules said, his smile slightly nervous. "Is that a good or bad thing?"

"Good, of course," Liam was quick to add, a lot more nervous but better at hiding it. "My sister only remembers good people."

I raised my eyebrow at him as I hugged him, and pointed to their assigned seats. Across from mine, and beside each other, at the Greek restaurant he chose for us. Liam was rarely in NV Park but he was very specific about his food and evening plans. I was lucky I got to choose where I sat.

"Where's your boy?" he asked me.

"Washroom."

Gio really had just stepped out, like thirty seconds before Liam and Jules arrived. Fortunate, because that gave me thirty seconds to breathe and pull myself together. I ended up *not* saying anything to Gio about the internet, because he was so pleasantly oblivious as usual. And when he started talking about something interesting he'd read about new cruelty-free pigments, I couldn't change the topic.

He did notice that I was off, a little jittery.

"Should I be worried about meeting your brother?" he'd asked.

Yes, but not for the reason he was thinking of, likely.

When he sauntered back to our table, there should have been no reason for him to worry. Gio Mella had everything going for him. He was young, attractive, intelligent. He wore that shirt and those pants like they served him. And he liked me. That should have been enough, for someone else, another time.

But he was also Gio Mella.

"This is Gio," I said, clearing my throat. "Gio, this is my brother Liam, and his date Jules."

Then they were all standing up and shaking hands. I did not miss the look Liam sent straight at me, silent but sharp, because Liam knew these things. He followed entertainment news, fashion, and society, and Gio Mella was at one point uncomfortably at the intersection of all three.

My brother and I were close, despite the distance and my avoiding him a lot lately. Two years of intermittent hanging out didn't take away the tells that I could still detect. He would never have made a scene, never would have blurted out right there what he was actually thinking, so instead it was polite conversation. I was sure he was compiling a list of questions in his head.

Gio and Jules quickly found a common interest that wasn't a mine field—it was in fact chemistry (yay!) because Jules was actually in Chem Eng for one year before he shifted into liberal arts marketing. *How did that happen? When did you wake up?* and Jules launched into that story that I already knew, because I was in the background of his life when it was happening. I tuned out for a second, long enough to see that my phone had a message, from Liam.

Liam: *Gio Mella? Seriously?*

I blinked and saw him giving me that look. I swiped my phone to life and started typing.

Me: *You wanted to meet the guy I'm seeing.*

Liam: *Why are you seeing the guy who had a threesome on his girlfriend's birthday?*

Me: *There's an explanation.*

Liam: *There's always an explanation.*

"...and I was standing there scared shitless because I didn't read a single word. Not a word. And I thought, I might do this wrong and make stuff explode. Right?"

Liam and I laughed in unison, as we used to at this part of the leaving-chem eng story.

Gio shook his head. "Actually you wouldn't have."

"But still, that was when it hit me..."

My brother and I went back to our phones.

Liam: *Are you doing this to give our parents a heart attack?*

Me: *Not fair.*

Liam: *Or Tita Ara at least. But I understand if you want her to seize up.*

Me: *I'm not doing anything to anyone.*

Liam: *You know about it, right? You know what he did? I can send you links.*

Me: *I'm very aware of how the internet works.*

Liam: *This is what you want?*

Me: *Stop asking me that like it means anything.*

Liam: *You know what I mean. Is this what you are now?*

Me: *What do you mean by that?*

Liam dramatically swiped his phone shut, and put it closer to Jules and out of his own reach. It was a wise thing to do, not answer. He didn't get to call me whatever he'd been thinking.

Dinner continued as usual, because we could do that. Liam and I grew up in a somewhat repressed household and knew how to keep up appearances, knew how to be "fine" without being fine. Only an expert in Iris and Liam Len-Larioca would have noticed that we were distant, our jokes were dry, and all we did was help the conversation along and weren't completely in it.

Maybe Jules would have known, because of their history.

Maybe Gio noticed, but didn't know Liam enough to figure out what it was.

In any case, the dinner was over in two hours and I let it end, and kissed my brother's cheek when I said goodbye.

"You sure?" Gio said. "You don't want to move to a coffee shop or something? I mean, we live here. No traffic."

"Liam needs to go," I said.

"I need to go," my brother said.

We watched them leave, and I wished I had been in a better mood. I wished that Liam had been a better brother. This was so interesting to me, the fact that Jules was around, and that they could be something. I wish I could have asked him about it.

"What do you want to do?" Gio asked. "It's still early."

I had a headache, but I also didn't give a shit anymore about a lot of things. "We need to talk about something," I told him.

"CAN YOU HAND ME THAT ONE?"

"This one?" Frankly, everything in the pile he was pointing to looked the same to me.

"Yeah, that one."

Gio's response to having just been told that his name was being taken in vain on the internet again, and seeing the evidence of it himself, was to ask if I wanted to work on the puzzle. That wasn't code for anything; it really was *working on the puzzle*.

There was significant progress since I'd last seen it. More of the sunset and orange sky. The pieces weren't in his neatly-organized piles according to color though, so someone must have messed it all up.

"Are we going to talk about it?" I asked him. Because I wasn't sure. After maybe ten minutes of watching him match pieces into the sky I wasn't sure if that was it, if we were going to pretend that we didn't know and none of it mattered.

His eyes lifted from the pool table, met mine. "You want to tell me now or later?"

"Tell you what?"

"That you're done with me."

Oh, he was being cute. "What?"

"I'm hoping you won't, because I'm totally capable of—"

"I'm not giving you a talk to break up!"

"What did you want to talk about?"

I blinked. "This doesn't bother you at all?"

"Of course it does. But I already told you everything, and none of this is new. But maybe...maybe you have something to say to *me*."

Wait. This turned how? "I only meant that if you're concerned about what anyone said about you—"

He shook his head. "Of course I am, but it's the same old bullshit that shouldn't have anything to do with me."

"It's you and it's also me, when people can't stop watching you."

"I know and I'm sorry. It's not going to end." His hand tightened around the puzzle piece he was holding. "Did you see anything you consider libelous?"

He didn't have to explain. I had a feeling we knew a lot more than we wanted to about libel and our legal options. "Nothing I'd pay a lawyer to chase."

"Did you see anything that made you feel bullied?"

All of it? And on his behalf? "The worst of it is about you."

"Yeah, and I don't care what nameless people are saying. But you do."

What do you need, Gio? He couldn't live like this. I didn't think I could live like this either, being the one connected to the noise while he retreated to his cave—or his puzzle—whenever he needed to. This wasn't right, was it? Where was the line I shouldn't cross? How far do I push and no further?

"I'm not breaking up," I said, never mind that we never really talked about being together. "But this is me they're talking about too. Again."

"I can't make them stop."

"I don't expect you to. But is there something else to the plan apart from hiding up here forever?"

"It's going to go away," Gio said, but also to himself as much as to me. "They'll go on a spree but it'll slow down and then go away. It always does."

What do you need, Gio? In five hundred words or less.
What do you need from him, Iris?

"I'm going back to my room," I said. "I'm not sure where this is going."

"This" was the immediate conversation at hand. What was I supposed to feel, when one of the few people who understood what it felt like to be shamed and hated by strangers was telling me to forget about it? Let it slide? But I didn't know what I expected him to say either.

"Hey, wait, don't go." Gio caught up with me before I got into the elevator. "Wait. Please don't go."

"It's late and I live here."

"I know but it doesn't matter if we both live here. If you check out on me, that's it. We—we won't be anything. Don't go."

Then what, Gio? I needed to go because I needed silence too. And maybe time to think, because I wasn't exactly sure what I wanted to hear.

"I'll pick you up tomorrow. Early morning. Let's go to... let's go to Manolo's thing."

Yeah, that wasn't what I was expecting to hear either. "Excuse me?"

"The family gathering tomorrow is Manolo's. It's not just one of those Sunday Country Club things they do that I never go to anymore. It's an engagement party."

"Oh. Wow." I barely knew Kimmy but this had to have been a huge step for her. Gio had to have known too.

"Yeah. I didn't want to go because that's how I am now, I don't go. But maybe—if you were there with me?"

"I don't need to go to meet your family, if that's what you think—"

"That's not what this is, I promise. Manolo and Kimmy are good people. I should be at their party."

Gio said that with the earnestness that went with everything he did.

"Only if you really want to be there," I relented.

"I want to be there with you," Gio said. "If I'm going to be there at all."

Close enough?

"How early?" I asked.

TWENTY-TWO

The other kind of really horrible alarm clock was the phone call from the ex-boyfriend.

"Iris."

"I know why you're calling, Bradley."

Because nothing else would have been cause for a four a.m. phone call. Seriously, some things about Bradley I still knew like no one else. He'd be mindful of time zones and wait to bother a person about a favor, or a death in the family, but any kind of internet humiliation was reason to hit the speed-dial and now.

"I don't understand how this happened."

"It's not so complicated. I'm seeing someone. That's all."

"But why...? Why are you seeing someone like him? I don't get it."

"You don't get to say anything about that."

"Fuck, Iris. Come on."

After everything that had already happened, *this* was what registered as potentially humiliating to me. Getting an early-morning lecture from my exhibitionist ex-boyfriend on what was proper behavior.

Dear God. Make it stop.

"If I stay absolutely quiet and let you talk, will you make it quick and shut up?" I said.

He groaned, in that way he did, I was sure of it. "I thought you were doing fine."

"I am."

"This doesn't look like you're fine."

"I don't know. You've been living in America for two years and suddenly you're an expert—explain what fine's supposed to look like."

"I'm not trying to argue. Anyone would be concerned. After what happened, no one wants you to be talked about like this again."

"Like what, Bradley?"

"Don't make me say it."

"But you called. You obviously want to."

"I'm concerned."

"You don't get to be anymore."

"You really want to do that? Don't. Not after everything we've been through."

Everything we've been through. Everything that happened. Everything, including the little times we betrayed each other, though not intentionally, but still destructively.

"Bradley," I said. "Your concern is noted. Now let me go back to sleep."

"Iris."

"What."

"Do you need help?"

"I *have* been getting help. Are you getting help? Apart from leaving, your favorite solution to things."

"That's not fair."

"No, Brad. What's not fair is that I stay here, I get the therapist, I come to terms with my pain, I get my self-esteem back, and then *you* get to call me from your hiding place in Wherever, USA to tell me what I'm doing is wrong. Do you get how shitty that is?"

There was a pause. Of course he didn't, until someone said it. Because no one ever said it.

"I'm sorry," he said. "You know I only want you to be okay."

"And I want *you* to be okay," I said. "I don't agree with how you did things but fine, whatever gives you the courage to step out with your head held up. Right?"

"Iris."

"You don't have to agree with me."

I didn't even end the call. The phone dropped from my hand, bounced off the edge of my bed and went over, and I didn't pick it up. Didn't want to. Gio's own coping mechanism could be strange but I understood why he did it. That damned thing was also the fastest way for old ghosts to resume their haunting.

GIO APOLOGIZED FOR EVERYTHING. The borrowed car (Damon's again), the fact that the "family gathering" was apparently in Tagaytay and a little further out than I'd realized, and for being a bundle of nerves because this was the first time he was seeing these people in months.

He was also preemptively apologizing for them.

"My mother will make some comment about your outfit," Gio was saying. "And you shouldn't take it seriously.

That's her making conversation, and when she offers to show you a designer or some store you should say yes and then don't worry about it, she'll never actually take you up on it. My dad...my dad will find some reason to ask you about your family. Who you're connected to. If he's golf buddies with anyone you're related to."

"My dad doesn't golf."

"Doesn't matter, he'll make you go through your entire family tree to find someone he possibly knows. Because that's the only way he can relate to people."

"I think I'll be okay."

"I have a cousin who likes to hit on the girlfriends. He just does. He thinks it's funny. He'll go as far as try to hook up with someone's girlfriend in a closet and then he'll brag about it at dinner. And another cousin, she'll try to get you alone and bait you to tell her mean things about me."

My family wasn't so great either, but wow, I was trying not to break into sleepy laughter at all of this.

There were cousins. Aunts. Uncles. Family friends, present at nearly every family gathering despite not being family. The one who liked to speak only in Spanish. The one who jerks off in the nearest bathroom after lunch. It was a spectacular list, and I didn't envy any part of having to keep track of this.

The tension between us was still there. I wish I could have done something to get rid of it but that conversation felt like pulling at a loose thread on a sweater. If only I knew what to ask of him. With Bradley it was easy—he was presenting me a life I didn't want. So I said I didn't want it.

I wasn't sure what this was. I mean, this was a very pleasant limbo, for as long as we didn't let the world in. But I wanted to be back in the world.

That was the point of the New Normal.

I also lacked sleep so I asked if I could do that.

I missed the entrance to the country club, because I was sleeping. It wasn't even their "regular" country club, Gio explained, which was in the city, but this was where they went during the summer. Even from inside the car I felt the chill in the Tagaytay air, and the hint of the view downhill from where we were, peeking from the trees that lined the area designated as parking.

So pretty, and only for parking.

Gio looked like he wanted to be somewhere else.

"Hey," I said. "Do you want to throw up?"

What do you need, Gio? Why are you even here? Was it me? Because I'd wanted to walk out on him? Because if he wasn't ready, he shouldn't be here.

"I'm fine," Gio said. "You know how it is. Family reunions."

"Mine aren't as fancy."

"The thing with big places like this is that there are many places to hide."

I made myself smile. "We're good at that, aren't we?"

TO CELEBRATE Kimmy Domingo and Manolo Mella's engagement, the Mella family threw an exclusive "breakfast to dinner" party at their Tagaytay country club for one hundred of their close friends. The Domingo and Mella family considered themselves the closest; Kimmy and Manolo's moms went to school together and were lifelong friends.

We arrived at the "breakfast" portion of the festivities, and were greeted upon entry to the clubhouse reception with matching shell necklaces and sparkling peach juice.

"Each pair of necklaces is a specific shade in the orange spectrum," the bubbly greeter explained to me. "Only two of a kind, in the entire party. Enjoy your day of love!"

"Oh my god," I whispered to Gio as we walked back out into the sunny garden. "She's not kidding, is she?"

"My mother does things this way."

"It's all very intense." At the same time, I had to appreciate it all. The summer country club resembled resort hotels I'd visited, maybe a few I'd gone to with the ex, but maybe it was different if the entire establishment existed to be at your service. People painting shells a specific shade of orange. Making you peach juice.

There was a small group of people in the garden, all guests, all indeed wearing a necklace in a shade different from ours.

"Giovanni," someone called. "Our prodigal son."

Gio froze, and he downed his juice like it was a shot of something stronger. Then he turned around and something about him switched on. "Dad."

Oh. Oh. Gio's dad was exactly like him, but older him. Future him. I could see where Gio would go gray, which parts of his body would get heavier, sturdier. They were even the same height. His dad was *not* wearing a necklace and instead of a fluted glass he was holding a bottle of beer.

"And please introduce me to your guest," he said, looking at me.

"This is Iris," Gio said. "My girlfriend."

I was? "Nice to meet you, sir," I said, offering my hand.

Mr. Mella shook it, like we were professionals, but he was still eyeing us with curiosity. "The pleasure is mine, Iris. What's your family name?"

"Len-Larioca. My name is Iris Len-Larioca."

"Is your family from Cebu?"

"No, sir."

"If you want to call me anything, call me *tito*, not sir. What do you do, Iris?"

"I work for a foundation."

He sipped from the bottle and urged me on. "I'll need more than that, you know. Since you're my son's girlfriend and all. What does the foundation do, Iris?"

"Oh, we give scholarships to female students who want to study STEM."

"Interesting. In the Philippines or abroad?"

"Both, depending on the grant."

"And is that working out?"

"Um, excuse me?"

"Do you get good students, send them to good schools?"

I nodded. I knew I should be speaking for my work more eloquently than this, but I was also meeting my *boyfriend's* dad. "Yes, yes, to everything."

"That's admirable," Mr. Mella said. He gave his son a light tap on the back. "It's nice to meet people who do good things for a living, right? Gio thinks all we do is make women feel insecure about their looks."

Gio rolled his eyes. "I said that *once* years ago."

"This is my serious son," Mr. Mella quickly added, laughing. "Always so serious. You probably like serious men, if you're putting up with our Giovanni."

"Dad." The sound came out like a warning.

"Well. It's too early in the morning for Giovanni's moods. Why don't you take her to the party, Gio, before you run out of the good tables."

"I thought this was the party…?" I started to say.

Gio shook his head. "No, this is the welcome area for the party. We still have to take a trip down." And he brushed past his dad, taking me with him, to wherever this party was supposed to be. "I'm sorry about that."

"You don't have to keep apologizing. I wasn't offended."

"You don't know them. Snide is their second language."

I thought I knew what snide was, like when an internet troll called me a whore. But to grab a transcript of that entire exchange and find the offensive message meant for me only between the lines? That was advanced snide.

Or imagined snide.

"I think I'm just going to take his word for it, that he doesn't hate me," I muttered.

The path to the party was literally a path. Uneven stones set against a bed of perfectly-level grass, leading slightly downhill.

"Of course he doesn't hate you," Gio was saying, keeping his voice low. "He won't have a problem with you at all. I'm the disappointment."

"In my family, the disappointments don't get welcomed to the party with necklaces."

"You don't know them." It sounded snappish, and at me.

"I get that." And I sounded snappish right back! It had to be because we were suddenly boyfriend and girlfriend. The transition to bickering couple was instant.

The path became stone steps up a small platform and whatever I was adding to that disappeared.

We were about to ride a cable car. This was a freaking cable car station, and when I followed the row of small cars my line of sight dropped, and the view was gorgeous lake and hills, but also, damn. Cable cars.

"Two of them! Thank god. Get in so we can leave now."

My body followed the voice on command, like an obedient person who didn't belong in this place. I'd taken two steps and then stopped because Gio had grabbed my arm and tried to keep me in place.

"We'll take the next one," he said.

"Oh, come on. It's just a few minutes. Unless you're afraid."

Against my better judgment I stepped forward, against my host and guide's wishes. Only because my mood was off, and I was being a rebel in the worst way.

So that was how we ended up in a tiny cable car with Leslie Tracy Rivera and her sister Vana.

TWENTY-THREE

The thing with celebrities, I noticed—some of them were better-looking in person.

My friend Bessy used to work in advertising, and when she was new at her job and in charge of going through audition videos, she mentioned that it was the strangest thing, when an actor or model was better-looking in person. Some people, she said, had a charm to them that the camera never seemed to properly catch. They'd be absolutely gorgeous when you saw them, and disappear into a crowd when filmed.

Based on what I'd read of Leslie Tracy Rivera's career, it seemed like she was always struggling. On the brink of stardom but never really there. She'd get a break and lose momentum, and then somehow find herself back with a new story and another push. Now I knew why. She was stunning in person; her skin and eyes sparkled from within. This didn't appear at all in her publicity photos or her TV shows or movies.

Then you had people like Vana and me, and Gio, whose videos or photos weren't created with the purpose of looking good or decent. We always, always looked better in person. It wasn't hard to look better than your nude video or photo when you had clothes or makeup on. When you didn't have something in your mouth.

The cable car setup was two benches, facing each other. Gio and I took the side facing downhill. Leslie was right in front of me, Vana across him. I was still holding my cute glass with a sip of juice left inside, and now I didn't know where to put it. Three out of four people in this cable car were very uncomfortable.

Vana Rivera looked gleeful.

"Gio Mella," she said, her smile wide enough for me to count her teeth if I wanted to. "Isn't this just perfect. We have a lot of catching up to do. And you're Iris?"

I nodded.

"Of course you are. We read stuff on the internet too. Not like this stud over here."

"Vana." Gio was not happy, but on a different frequency of stressed from when he talked to his dad. "Can you not."

"It's a ten-minute ride down. What else are we going to do?"

Leslie rolled her eyes and pressed against the glass, as much as she could. Then she looked at me, really looked at me. "I'm Leslie," she said.

"Yeah, I know that too."

"See, this is what I love about you guys," Vana continued, determined to be the cable car circus ringmaster. "This is what I keep telling you, Gio. Go with it. Explore those sexual urges and do it safely, with people you can trust. They don't teach you that in sex ed."

"Nobody teaches that," Leslie snapped.

"Well maybe they should. Protect yourself, set your

limits, find someone you trust, don't hurt people. Look at me, sex ed teacher."

Vana Rivera was beautiful in a different way from her sister. They might have resembled each other but Vana's personality filled the car, possibly spilled out of it into the ravine we were traveling over. There was also a joy to her that Leslie did not have. None of us had it, because damn, this was awkward.

Gio's sexual history was in this cable car.

I wouldn't be surprised if Vana's friend, the other part of that threesome, was somewhere on the premises too.

"So what's your button, Iris?" Vana asked me.

"My what?"

"Don't answer that," Gio said.

"Don't tell her what to do, Gio," Vana scolded. "I have a feeling Iris knows what I'm talking about. We're in a sisterhood now, whether she likes it or not. Iris. What's the button?"

What's the button.

What's my thing.

Why did you take a video of yourself?

Do you like to watch yourself, Iris?

"I like to watch myself. Sometimes."

I said that. The words came out of my mouth.

Gio and Leslie stopped pretending to look somewhere else.

Vana rubbed her hands together.

"In what way?" she said. "Like you're another person in the room?"

I nodded. "Sometimes. But more often…like I'm seeing myself through his eyes."

"The guy who's having sex with you?"

"Yeah."

"Like, as he's having sex with you? You want to see yourself as he sees you? When you're coming?"

It was better to look at Vana and close in on her, and not have to think about the others there with us. I'd opened the can of worms, anyway. Worms all over the place.

"Not exactly that," I corrected. "Not just that. I want to be everywhere. See him and me. Like, if I could switch back and forth at will."

Vana leaned forward, nodding. "I get it. I get it. You ever tried doing POV video?"

"No...we didn't get to do that."

"You mean you and your ex."

"No videos for me for a very long time, thanks."

"That's too bad." Vana shrugged and leaned back against her seat again. "But that's interesting. Like... switching exhibitionist and voyeuristic tendencies. Or simultaneous. I get why Gio would satisfy you. He tends toward exhibitionist too. You *are* satisfying her in the ways she needs you to, aren't you, G?"

"Oh my god," Leslie said. "*Ate*, please stop."

Vana raised an eyebrow, but continued to address only me. "It never would have worked out between these two. Les here believes her purity hype. You can't retroactively be pure if you've already sucked dick."

"Bitch," Leslie said.

"Yeah, pure people don't call people bitches either. Iris, I'm glad we met. I hope you and G stay happy for a long time. And if you want to try a woman or need someone to hold the camera, you know who to call."

I didn't know what to say to that.

The cable car paused, swung lightly, and then stopped.

"Well, now the ride's over," Vana announced. "Wasn't that so much fun for everyone."

GIO HAD his dad's eyes. Made sense. They were not completely out of place in this crowd, not that they were all fair-skinned and blue-eyed, but because everyone looked different. Different didn't hold anyone back, as long as they could afford to look as good as they felt.

There were indeed more people at the real party and they had already begun eating breakfast. I smelled bacon and pancakes, saw bowls of *champorado*, fresh fruit on plates. I hadn't had a bite to eat but didn't feel hungry at all.

"Iris." My boyfriend nudged me, distracting me from my ogling.

"What?"

"We should talk about it."

Almost instinctively, we walked toward an empty spot, under one of several archways that would lead guests inside. Different on the outside was not the same as different on the inside, and we knew how to find the quiet places, where we'd be free to talk.

"I don't feel like talking about it," I told him.

"Is it true? What you told Vana?"

I sighed. "Why would I lie?"

"Did you want people to see the video? Is that why you took it?"

Did he just ask me that? I wasn't sure. I waited, hoping I'd misheard.

He was looking at me, waiting for an answer. So perhaps I hadn't misheard, and he'd actually suggested that I *wanted* strangers to watch me have sex.

Was that what he was asking? Did I want the video to get out? Did I want random strangers to watch me at my most vulnerable, to leer at me like they knew every inch of my body? Did I want pervs to think they had a chance with me because of what they'd seen?

Did I ask for the past two years of my life?

Did I deserve what I got?

Was that what he was suggesting?

"Of course not." My voice trembled with anger. "I can't believe you'd even ask. What I said in that cable car was something I thought I was sharing with people who wouldn't judge me."

"I only thought...but wouldn't people seeing you be exciting? To someone who had that kink."

"Did you have sex with two women at the same time just to prove to people that you can?"

"What? No."

"Did you bring me here to prove that you can have all this sex now because you didn't for years?"

Anger began to flare up in him, I could see it. "No."

"Then you know how boneheaded your question was. Give me some credit. There are things you do with people you trust and what happened to me was a violation of that. I can't believe I'm explaining this to *you*."

"To me? Why do you think I'd automatically understand everything?"

Because he had done so well so far.

Or did I imagine it all? Did I hope too much that I'd found the only person I'd feel safe with?

Was I wrong? Dear God. I'd told him *everything*. I showed him everything. There was nothing left of me to discover.

Someone yelled a little too loudly for her pancakes and Gio remembered where we were. "I don't want to fight here."

"Oh, we're not going to." I pushed my empty glass onto his chest. "See you later, boyfriend."

I started walking away. My sandals made no noise against the perfect grass. I didn't know where to go so I simply walked where the people weren't, and that led to a small stairwell inside the pavilion that I thought might go to a bathroom, but it didn't.

It just kept winding down, and the smell of food disappeared. I found myself on yet another lower floor of this place, a foyer with couches surrounded by closed doors. But it was empty and that was enough.

No cellphone signal. Only faint sounds of birds chirping.

This was enough.

THE WOMAN of the hour was the next human being I saw, by accident, when an hour later she wandered in because this was apparently the bedroom where she had stayed the night.

"You're here!" Kimmy said. And then, after a longer look at me, "You don't want to be here."

I had to agree.

Her eyes went up, to nothing in particular, just the general direction of the party upstairs. "You'll need an exit. There's a service road that goes all the way down to this part of the country club. I'll call the driver and have you picked up there. Do you want to be driven to NV Park?"

"Kimmy, I'm sorry," I said. "It's a lot to ask. I'm sorry for—"

"Don't apologize," she said. "You do what you need to

do. This is not the healthiest place for people; I know it more than anyone."

She reached for a phone screwed to the wall, and gave instructions for someone to get us at the guest lodge. "Five minutes," she told me. "And you might want to tell him to drive through somewhere. You haven't eaten?"

"No. Um, congrats on the engagement party?"

Kimmy laughed. "We're already married. They don't know."

"Oh. Wow. Wow."

"Yeah." Kimmy smiled, and she looked happy. "Very small ceremony last week. None of these clowns were there."

"You're not going to tell them?"

She put an arm around me and we began to walk down a hall, toward another exit I hadn't even seen. "One of the accidental privileges of not giving a fuck is that I get to decide what people see. Matilda likes closure, right? Because she's like that. She wants a certain status quo maintained. Poetic justice. I think we all reach that point but in different ways."

We went through a white gate, into a dirt road. There was a black SUV there already. I saw my reflection on its tinted window and saw the orange necklace, the one that Gio had the only match to. I touched the shiny shell and almost took it off.

"What do you want me to tell Gio?" Kimmy asked.

"Nothing," I said.

TWENTY-FOUR

"Sleepover!" Matilda said, when I showed up at her door with an overnight bag of clothes and my laptop.

"How long can I stay?"

"As long as you need to."

"What's your Wi-Fi password?"

Easy as that, when it came to finding relocation space. It was harder, the first time I ran away. That I kept going back to the same house for as long as I did, and shared space with people who were ashamed of me, was now unthinkable. The ninth floor was as much his home as mine, and I couldn't stay there until I'd figured out how to talk to him.

Matilda's was a temporary solution, one that had decent broadband and smelled of floral essential oils most of the time. Not bad.

"You're not going to move out, are you?" she asked me, at breakfast, on day two.

"No," I said. "I like it here."

"Good. You know how I feel about that. Don't let him chase you away."

Breakfast at Matilda's meant toast and fancy jam, also a

winner in my book. By then I also discovered something about her routine that she never let on before.

She worked. From home, in flowy butterfly-print robes, but it was work nonetheless. Her laptop was stationed so she could look out the window, and there was a document open. She wasn't constantly online so the screen would show the same document when she left her seat. I didn't want to ask her what she did—living in her home already seemed like Too Much Information. It didn't look like she was writing it though, so maybe it was something she was reviewing or editing.

This was what she did, I assumed, in between trips to the pool area.

We talked a little about Kimmy and Manolo's wedding. Matilda and Mosh were witnesses ("best BISHes"), but apparently only found out on the day of the wedding. A civil ceremony of less than ten people, then drinks after. The bride wore red. No one was allowed to talk about what had happened. When Gio and I visited Manolo at the motel photo shoot, he was married by then. Gio didn't get the memo either, most likely.

I couldn't imagine doing something like that, but yeah, that was an intense family.

The email alerts kept coming, but only trickled in. Whoever was tipping off the sites obviously didn't get an invite to Sunday's engagement party. The idea that someone would have gotten a photo of that cable car ride was strange but I was also curious. Because damn it, for all the silly jumping to conclusions about us, nothing could have beat that. That would have lit up the blog for days.

But no one picked it up, so that juicy tidbit went unnoticed.

Too bad for you all.

I wondered what other crazy things happened to other people that we never got to see.

By day three I needed to replenish my clothes and supplies. I did a run early in the morning, thinking that was the best time not to run into Gio. Upon entering my apartment I stepped on five notes, folded, all his handwriting, and I almost laughed because for all the romance of old-fashioned correspondence, it was also easy to ignore. And throw away. Or at least, pushed into a corner with one foot.

I saw it, but I didn't see it.

On day four of living with Matilda, the email alerts stopped. The activity on the original blog posts ended—no new comments.

Gio was the object of internet scorn for under nine days this time, and then the people moved on. Again.

"It's because of that model's dick pic. You wanna see?" Matilda explained, with that helpful offer, which I refused. "You know it's better when there's no blur."

There was one new message I did get, a chaser at the end of a sour cocktail.

Liam: *Do you want to see?*

Me: *Of course I do.*

And within seconds, I received it. A forwarded email, sent again by Tita Ara, to her family and dozens of friends.

DEAR DARLINGS,

I HAVE DECIDED, for my own peace as I continue to age, to forgive. I have decided that as much as we try, sometimes a person just resists the good path, and when they do that, we at some point must accept that they will learn the consequences of their actions.

Our dear Iris has always been a handful, and maybe it's time to let her live her life, with our good wishes. Knowing that we will welcome her back wholeheartedly if she decides to turn away from those influences. To do the right thing.

ARA

I TEXTED LIAM. *WTF?*

Liam: *She's here right now. At home. They're talking about forgiveness and shit.*

Me: *When did she find out about the new thing?*

Liam: *Yesterday. She hasn't left. They talked about you for hours and hours.*

Me: *I thought she forgave me.*

Liam: *That's what she said.*

"I guess it's safe to go out again," I joked, returning to my place in Matilda's world. "I got word that my family 'forgives' me."

We were talking over dinner. Well, while I had dinner on day four, while she picked at a bowl of grapes and sat on the sofa.

"It was always safe for you to go out," Matilda scoffed.

"You know what I mean."

"I don't know what you mean. Do you mean, is the ninth floor safe for occupancy?"

My fork didn't have any food on it when I bit it. "Yeah. Well. He can't make me talk to him if I don't want to."

"Why don't you want to again?"

"I don't know what to say."

"Yeah," Matilda said, "you said that, on Monday. You would have had days to come up with a new answer."

Not for lack of trying. I thought about a lot of things, at night, in the shower, at my desk at work, everywhere. I missed him, but then asked myself if I should hate myself for missing him. Because if I opened the door to him again, this would happen. It would keep happening even if I didn't give a shit.

Was it healthy for me to keep fighting?

What do you need, Iris?

"You know what you need?" Matilda said, eerily.

I nodded. "I think I need to go back home."

LIAM: *Right now?*

Me: *Yeah.*

Liam: *But it's late.*

Me: *I don't care.*

BY THE TIME I got to the home I grew up in, it was late. It was strange to be at that doorstep again, with the same overnight bag I took with me when I left, and the same one I'd taken to Matilda's.

It wasn't even real luggage or anything. It was a big tote, but sturdy, with reinforced lining, and a zipper. I could carry days' worth of clothing and supplies in there and nothing would spill out. The move to NV Park was the result of planning, but when I did move out, it was quick and dramatic, with shouting and crying. This tote was perfect for throwing stuff into and then storming off in a huff.

Nighttime at home wasn't very quiet. Dad watched the news. Mom would be on the phone with Tita Ara, if not speaking to her right there in the house. Liam would be coming in from some dinner before midnight.

Maybe they knew I was coming, because the house was bright and noisy all right, but I felt the heavy anticipation.

They should have known I would show up, after they announced it.

That I had been forgiven.

Liam was watching me from when I had gotten into the front gate and was responsible for pulling me into the house.

"I'm sorry for being a bitch," he said. "But why are you here? What happened?"

I hugged him. "I had the strangest time with someone else's family."

"All families are strange. You know that?"

"Some stranger than others?" God it felt good to hug him again. "Liam, I miss you. I miss knowing you're across the hall if I need you for something. I need that in my life again."

"Sis, I've missed you more."

"So are you seeing Jules?"

"I always see Jules."

"You know what I mean."

"That deserves a long story with drinks and steak."

I checked the time. "Maybe not tonight then."

"Are you really coming in?"

"Of course."

Like before, right? Like when Liam told me to come back in, I'd already spent too much time outside. Except he didn't look comforted or relieved; he knew as well as I did that this wasn't over.

My parents and my aunt were in the dining room. No surprise—it was always where at least one of them was, at any time of the day.

"Good evening," I said.

When I was younger, we joked about these three people being shapes. My dad was a square, my mother a rectangle, Tita Ara an oval. Liam and I would draw them as those, with hair on top and shoes at the bottom. Maybe a handbag for the oval. Those basic shapes were still visible in a way, but time seemed to have...shrunk them? Did that happen?

"Iris." It was Tita Ara who spoke first. She always did. Liam and I also liked to speculate on the epic favor she must have done for my parents when they were younger, for her to get the position of power like this and for so long. No one else talked about it because Ara Len-Larioca had always been the queen bee of their lives and they never questioned it.

"Tita Ara," I said.

Sometimes I still had dreams about this. About coming home, and the kind of welcome I'd get. Would I get hugs and happy tears? Would someone throw a plate at me? Would someone pull my hair?

I didn't think of this being so...quiet.

I guess I had to speak up.

"Someone sent me the email you wrote," I told them. "Just now, actually. I wanted to come over right away."

A familiar look came over my aunt's face. *Of course you would,* it seemed to say. She always did fancy herself an expert on us, on every single member of this family, an expert on everything we needed.

My mom and dad lived by what she decided they needed. They were waiting for her cue, even now.

"I dropped by to say that I forgive you, too," I said.

"Forgive *me*?" Tita Ara recoiled. "You're something else, aren't you? I thought—I thought in time you would have humbled. Seems like you take after your dad in many things."

My dad, Ara's younger brother, stood up at this. "*Ate.*"

"No," because she wasn't done yet, "Iris, after all that you put your family through. How dare you come here and say you forgive *me*. After everything we tried to do for you. You ungrateful harlot."

My mother gasped. My father might have too, if he were the type who did that.

But Tita Ara wasn't the first person to call me that, though maybe her choice of words was more creative. I was pleased to discover that the word or the anger behind it no longer made me instantly dissolve into tears. Even when delivered by one of the persons closest to me.

This was starting to feel right.

I only needed one short breath to get myself ready for the next thing. "Yes, I forgive you. I don't know why you treated me that hurtful way, but I understand it. You're fiercely protective, and you're protecting something you know is yours, in the way you know how. You cut me off so what's yours can survive, and I appreciate that now because I know I have to do the same."

"Wait," my mom spoke out of turn. It was never her turn when Tita Ara was around. "Wait. You're not coming home?"

I shook my head, but this time with confidence. "No."

"But...we said it's okay. It can still be okay, Iris. We can forget what happened just now."

They don't get it.

I didn't need to be around people who couldn't, wouldn't get it. Figuring it out was already such a task.

"It doesn't matter. But I'm glad you're beginning to think that it could be okay." I looked at each of them, at their faces that were beginning to change. "Thank you for sending that email, Tita Ara. I'll move on with no hard feelings, but I can't come back and act as if nothing happened. Maybe when you all accept that, we can talk again. But this is a step."

The familiar sound behind me was Liam. I knew he'd disappeared for a bit and came back, and heard most of what I'd said. The older people in the room were still in shocked silence as I turned around and headed out.

"I'll drive you back," Liam said. "And I got these from your room."

I peeked into the paper bag he had and it was some things I had left behind in the rush of running away. That good pair of jeans. Those purple flats. That favorite old shirt. Unused notebooks.

"You knew I wasn't going to be staying," I said.

"Your bag's empty," he said.

It was; I didn't come armed with old baggage. I came to rescue a few treasured things, one last time.

TWENTY-FIVE

Friday was Miley's last day at work.

She wasn't leaving for Geneva just yet, but there were things to do before going on a great new adventure. Like shopping for a completely new wardrobe. And hopping off to a last, exquisitely long beach trip. As one does, when switching hemispheres.

By then I wasn't worried. I shouldn't be worried for another year anyway, she told me, at least until the Figueras patriarch did his annual evaluation of the subsidiaries and foundations. As long as we kept the lights on, she'd fight to keep us all employed.

"He should be happy," Miley said. "We got more new donors this year. And a new grant's opened up this week. We got the commitment yesterday."

"Maybe we're a new trend," I replied. "Female scientists, yay."

"Whatever the reason, I'm glad for the money."

We were in Miley's office, and it was a mess of boxes and personal items being sorted and packed up. I was not going to be moving into the room, even if I was taking over most of her work. I didn't feel it was right, and also, her dad was going to be appointing a consultant to be the credible older person because sometimes that was needed. That person would be occupying this room.

"Hey," she said. "Francine told me that you emailed her."

I did that yesterday. I had totally ignored the email Miley sent, providing Francine's contact info, but when I got to work a message from her was the first thing I saw. She was doing an anti-bullying seminar and needed input on something. It wasn't even a big deal, in the end. I quickly replied, agreed to see more of her material, and even maybe coffee if she needed more.

"Yeah," I answered. "I'm not ready to talk about myself yet, but she didn't need me to talk about myself."

"Francine's great. I should see her before I go."

"You should."

"Take my next meeting, will you?" Miley said. "Conference room right now. I don't want to do any other work thing today."

"Gotcha," I said. "What's this about?"

"Exploratory meeting with new donor corporation. There's an amount committed, so ask them how they want it allocated and spent. And maybe other miscellaneous agenda items."

I could do all of that, no problem. "Done and done."

Grabbing my notepad and a pen, I headed over to the conference room. Miley's two p.m. was there and ready to meet.

Miley's two p.m. was Gio Mella.

Gio Mella in a pressed shirt, a tie, a coat, dark pants, leather shoes.

"This is real," he said. "It's a real meeting, not a setup. I had a feeling they'd send you to talk to me."

What was he even doing here? Was he getting a job? Here? Was he—?

"Oh," I said, the most logical answer sinking in. "Your family's company is the donor?"

Gio nodded. "The family already has a foundation. I was able to get them to commit some of the money specifically for this."

"'This?'"

"Chemistry and chemical engineering scholarships. Research grants for ethical and sustainable cosmetics chemistry projects."

"You did this."

"Yes I did." Gio shifted in the leather chair, and it bounced softly. "It wasn't so hard, once I looked at the annual reports."

"It does make a lot of sense," I admitted. "As far as Bella Mariel Cosmetics is concerned, anyway. The benefits are obvious."

"How long is this meeting?"

"An hour."

"Can I tell you something now or do we have to do that later?"

I didn't want to talk about anything else at work but here we were and I couldn't be expected to draft a budget when certain things were unsaid. I wasn't a robot; I still had feelings. "Miscellaneous items."

"What?"

"My boss Miley said this meeting was about the new grant and miscellaneous items. So, sure. Say what you need to say."

My pen was quite accidentally poised over a blank

page. This was my work stance. Even on this conference table that could seat eight, I was in my usual chair, my usual spot. Straight back, pen ready.

"In five hundred words or less," I added.

That took him aback. "What?"

"We go for clear and concise in this room. Cut out the padding."

Gio suppressed a smile and placed his palms on the table. "Fine. I don't get to mess around and try again?"

"How many words is that already?"

"Fine."

He looked great, all cleaned up and serious.

"Iris, I had a thousand apologies ready for what happened in Tagaytay. For everything you saw, everything I said to you. Everything that everyone else said to you. I left some half-assed apologies under your door. You probably ignored them. Then I remembered that you've already told me a bunch of times that I apologize too much."

I had told him that, yes.

He continued, "Maybe that's been my problem, for a long time. I don't fit in there with my family. I feel that you might tell me to be happy that they accept me for who I am, because other families are so close-minded and harsh. I know that I'm lucky in many ways, that they have all this money, that they've given me so much, and that I can screw up so badly and not have any of that jeopardized."

"Yes, you are lucky."

"I know that. I want to keep that lucky streak going. Can I ask you a question now?"

"Me?"

"Yes. That happens in this room, right? You get asked questions too."

"Yes, I do."

"Do you think you will ever meet someone like me again?"

It was not the question I expected, and I laughed, and coughed. "That's what you ask me?"

The sly grin was slightly out of place on serious, cleaned-up Gio, but I liked it. I was beginning to recognize him again. "That's what I said. I understand why you want to dump me. I did the worst thing, the thing I said I never wanted to do. I hurt you again, and you shouldn't instantly forgive that. It takes a special kind of stupidity to find a new way to hurt you, and I found it. Damn it."

This was...he was right.

Gio continued, "I hope you're going to let me defend myself. Yes that was completely stupid, but I can learn. You know I can. But it's going to be a struggle, and I imagine there will be other shit. I have issues. My family's expensive excess baggage to carry around. You'll run into Vana and that can't be as fun as she makes it sound. I don't want to completely uproot myself and live somewhere no one knows me either. Like I said, I was lucky to have been born into that family and I've been trying to see how long I can live without the privileges, but this can't be permanent. I'm not ready for it."

"I don't see how that has anything to do with—"

"But you know all of this. You know because we told each other everything. So I wondered, how could I have screwed this up? Then I realized that you think I watched your video."

What?

He was watching my face and knew he had something. "You think I watched it. You think I watched it and knew everything you liked and still completely misunderstood you."

"But I gave it to you and gave you time to watch it."

"And then you left the room. I didn't watch it, Iris. I didn't know what you liked. I wasn't going to learn it seeing you with the guy who left. I...wanted to learn it for myself. I knew I'd do better."

I gasped. "You really are competitive."

He never saw it. What did this mean...? How did it change anything? It meant he knew but didn't see. The way I knew of his history but never saw. It didn't change that it happened, that we did things with other people, but at some point everyone would have history that they chose to hide or share. Trust was going to have to fill the gaps.

"You gave me a way to start over," I said.

"No," he said. "You did that for me first."

We could argue about this all day.

"I'm falling for you." His words spilled out. Padding cut. "I am. If you're worried about our other baggage—those other incidents—then we can talk about it and maybe work out anything that we need to work out about it, but I already know and I don't care. I'm falling anyway."

"Have you thought about why you maybe shouldn't?"

He pulled back sharply. "You interrupted me. And yes, of course, probably just as much as you think about me being the worst thing to ever happen to you."

This? This was what was bothering him?

"What a boneheaded thing to say," I told him. "You're not the worst thing."

He raised an eyebrow. "Do you think...you can still trust me?"

I liked to think that all the time I spent in this room, meeting people, and judging their sincerity and intentions, could tell me how to feel as he asked me this. But this wasn't work. This was my heart, my future.

I probably was never going to meet someone else like him again, soon.

"I can," I said.

"You think you can fall for me?"

"Well, yeah."

"How bad was this past week for you?"

He paused and maybe was waiting for a response. "It was bad," I admitted.

His face fell. "Because of me?"

Yes, and no. But it was all connected, and I had to accept that. "Because I thought I was over it, people calling me names. And people calling you names. I wish I could say I can't be affected by it. I keep thinking...what will my family say? I just found out that they've forgiven me, you know that? They'll take me back in if I agree that we erase what happened, move on as before. I don't suppose that offer will stand if I keep seeing you."

"So you're saying we're over."

I rolled my eyes. "I'm not saying that at all."

He frowned. "Maybe you need to cut the padding yourself then. Do you want to stay together or not?"

"I do," I said. That was nice. A loaded little phrase that was nonetheless pleasant. Peaceful, even. "I do. I want to stay together *anyway*, I was going to say, because screw what they say they want. Screw forgiveness on their terms. Screw acceptance that isn't really acceptance. I don't need that in my life."

"And me? You need me?"

That earned him one of my best fake scowls. "What do you want to hear, Gio?"

"Why you need me. Feel free to exceed five hundred words."

I was going to tease him some more about what a dumb

question that was, but no. It wasn't *so* dumb. He needed to hear it, and honesty was good to include as a daily habit for me. "You've seen the worst of it and somehow you're in here looking hot in that suit and I know how great we can be together."

"Oh." Gio looked at what he was wearing, pulled his coat together. "This is mine, you know. My own clothes."

"They look great. It doesn't hurt that you're here making sure more women study science."

"Doesn't hurt that this way I'm sure to find someone who can replace me in the company."

Of course. It made sense. I shrugged and pretended to write a note on the pad. *Applicant is practical and forward thinking. History of questionable decisions.*

Heart and mind in right place.

"So is that settled?" he asked.

"What's settled?"

His face tipped toward me, closer. Not enough to reach me. But enough to make the room seem smaller, and make me feel warm, and inappropriately tingly. "You, me, falling. Everything."

And finally: applicant's eyes are irresistible. Recommendation is not to resist.

"Yes. Settled. We are a go."

"Awesome." He leaned back and it was all business again. "What's next?"

"This." I tapped my pen against the notepad. "We actually do have to structure your grant. You ready to work, Gio?"

"Yes," he said. "Finally."

TWENTY-SIX

I'm running.

I'm running and I'm not stopping.

I'm running and my breaths are short but my lungs are strong, and my eye can't leave the ball, because it's the first time that I've been this close and you know what, I'm going for it.

There's a flash of color beside me, and then a gust of wind, and it's a person. A person who has taken the ball away from me. He's faster. I lose it because I hesitate, don't want to trip over myself and fall. It's my mistake.

I get angry and I let out a yell, and chase after him.

I'm chasing after him halfway across, and think I see an opening. It's not. I stick my foot out and it's wrong, and I fall.

He switches his angle and I lose him.

"You okay there?" Andrea stopped and offered her hand, pulling me up.

"I'm fine," I told her. "Not a bad fall."

"Didn't look it. But you never know. Oh, they got a goal."

Yeah, the guy I lost the ball to managed to get their first

goal in. The Saturday football game between Taylor Global's employees and NV Park's residents was now tied. I was there, on the actual field, and wearing Gio Mella's shirt while at it, because Gio himself was running late and no one wanted to forfeit. Even in the neighborhood they took this somewhat seriously, and I wanted to respect that passion (or was it needless intensity).

In any case, all that running around was actually fun. Endorphins, adrenaline, whatever was responsible for my rush and sudden competitive streak, thank you because I was having fun.

At halftime we retreated to our benches, and drank water. Then a message came in for me, on my phone.

Unknown number: *Sorry I'm late. Getting this took longer than I thought it would. Dropping off stuff at Tower 3 then there in a minute.*

Gio wasn't the only person I was getting sudden messages from. Through my brother, I knew that my mom *and* dad wanted to talk to me. Whenever I was ready, Liam said, and apparently without Tita Ara's presence this time. I hadn't been ready yet, but I knew I was going to be.

Inner peace was a good thing.

"Where's Mella?" Damon Esquibel demanded.

"I think he'll be here in a minute," I said, showing them, showing his friends, my phone. "I think he just texted me."

Damon, Andrea, Ethan, even Moira (Ethan's girlfriend who preferred not to play even under threat of calling off the game) began to applaud. "Hallelujah."

Within minutes, indeed, my boyfriend arrived. He ran the rest of the block and I could see him do it, see him running toward us.

"You have a freaking phone," I gasped, when he made it into the playing field. "I can't believe it."

He fished it out of his pocket. New phone, indeed. Still shiny, still covered in protective plastic. "Yeah, it was getting hard to date you without it."

"I can't believe you caved."

"Convenience isn't caving," he said. "And I like your voice. That's the only acceptable reason to get this."

"Fine. I'll accept that."

He noticed that I was sweaty and that I was wearing the Mella shirt, the very same one he refused to buy and wear from Damon. He turned to his friend with a big grin. "It looks better on her anyway."

"Just say you're fucking ready to play, Mella. No more excuses. Sit this one out, Iris, if you want to."

"Thank god!" I took him up on that. Happy hormones aside.

The break was over, but there was enough time for a kiss. Then he winked at me and ran toward the other players.

Sometimes I looked at him like this, from a distance, the same distance that strangers would have access to, and marvel at how little one could know about him from this vantage point. Fine, you could make assumptions about him based on what he wore that day, what his body looked like, which persons he smiled at when he got to the field.

How many of those assumptions would be wrong?

But even if you were wrong, so what.

And if you were looking, and you saw which girl he talked to, which sweaty girl he wrapped his arms around and kissed, kissed deeply, and happily, kissed like no one's business, you might have made assumptions about him also.

Maybe you would be right or wrong.

Maybe you would keep those assumptions to yourself and wish real people real happiness.

Maybe you would be a great person and I'd want you to be my friend, my confidante, part of my new normal.

Maybe I'd be that person for you, whatever your incident, whatever humiliation you're surviving from.

I was getting better at finding those people. If there was anything to cherish from the worst time of my life, it was that I developed that skill. Apart from it, there was nothing else to want, or need. For now.

The End

AUTHOR'S NOTE

Thank you for reading the Iris book. (It was a bit more difficult to write, let's be honest.)

Along the way this manuscript had an interesting detour–it was read and discussed at the 55th UP National Writers Workshop, in Laguna. It was a first for me, having my work looked at this way by academics, poets, *literary* people. I submitted *Iris*, wanting this different audience for a story that I felt was still me, but darker. By then the manuscript was finished and already with my editor, but at the workshop I felt I was there as my character, looking for people who'd accept her for who she was. I did find those people, by the way! Thank you to UPNWW for the chance to talk about romance, and the way I've been writing it.

Thank you: Aileen, Anna, Hannah, Sheila, Six, Layla, and Veronica. On the matters of therapy, counseling, legal consequences, chemistry, lipstick, cosmetics industry regulations, and various other things, they helped. Any errors are mine, or deliberate fudges for the sake of fiction.

Mina V. Esguerra

CHIC MANILA SERIES BY MINA V. ESGUERRA

Contemporary romances set in the Philippines. Can be read as standalones.

My Imaginary Ex (#1), Jasmine and Zack
Fairy Tale Fail (#2), Ellie and Lucas
No Strings Attached (#3), Carla and Dante
Love Your Frenemies (#4), Kimmy and Manolo
That Kind of Guy (#5), Julie and Anton
Welcome to Envy Park (#6), Moira and Ethan
What You Wanted (#7), Andrea and Damon
Iris After the Incident (#8), Iris and Gio
Better At Weddings Than You (#9), Daphne and Aaron

ABOUT THE AUTHOR

Mina V. Esguerra writes contemporary romance, young adult, and new adult novellas. Visit her website minavesguerra.com for more about her books, talks, and events.

When not writing romance, she is president of communications firm Bronze Age Media, development communication consultant, and indie publisher. She created the workshop series "Author at Once" for writers and publishers, and #romanceclass for aspiring romance writers. Her young adult/fantasy trilogy Interim Goddess of Love is a college love story featuring gods from Philippine mythology. Her contemporary romance novellas won the Filipino Readers' Choice awards for Chick Lit in 2012 (Fairy Tale Fail) and 2013 (That Kind of Guy).

She has a bachelor's degree in Communication and a master's degree in Development Communication.

Addison Hill series: Falling Hard | Fallen Again | Learning to Fall

Breathe Rockstar Romance series: Playing Autumn | Tempting Victoria | Kissing Day (short story)

Chic Manila series: My Imaginary Ex | Fairy Tale Fail | No Strings Attached | Love Your Frenemies | That Kind of Guy | Welcome to Envy Park | Wedding Night Stand (short story) | What You Wanted | Iris After the Incident | Better At Weddings Than You

Scambitious series: Young and Scambitious | Properly Scandalous | Shiny and Shameless | Greedy and Gullible

Interim Goddess of Love series: Interim Goddess of Love | Queen of the Clueless | Icon of the Indecisive | Gifted Little Creatures (short story) | Freshman Girl and Junior Guy (short story)

The Future Chosen

Anthology contributions: Say That Things Change (New Adult Quick Reads 1) | Kids These Days: Stories from Luna East Arts Academy Volume 1 | Sola Musica: Love Notes from a Festival | Make My Wish Come True | Summer Feels

Contact Mina

minavesguerra.com
minavesguerra@gmail.com

BOOKS BY FILIPINO AUTHORS
#ROMANCECLASS

romanceclass

Visit romanceclassbooks.com to read more
romance/contemporary/YA by Filipino authors.

Printed in Great Britain
by Amazon